FAR OUT
FAIRY TALES

STONE ARCH BOOKS
a capstone imprint

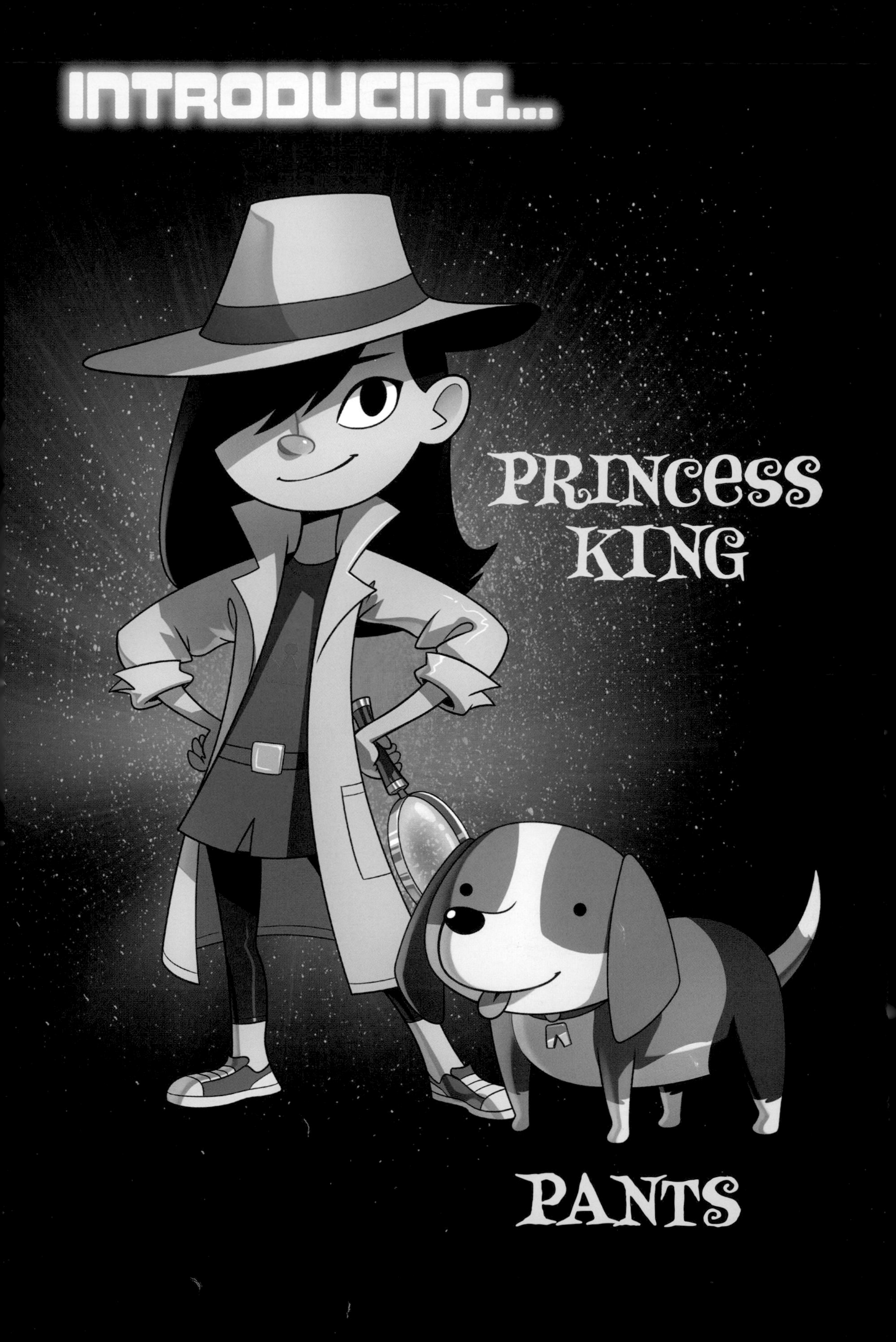
INTRODUCING...
PRINCESS KING
PANTS

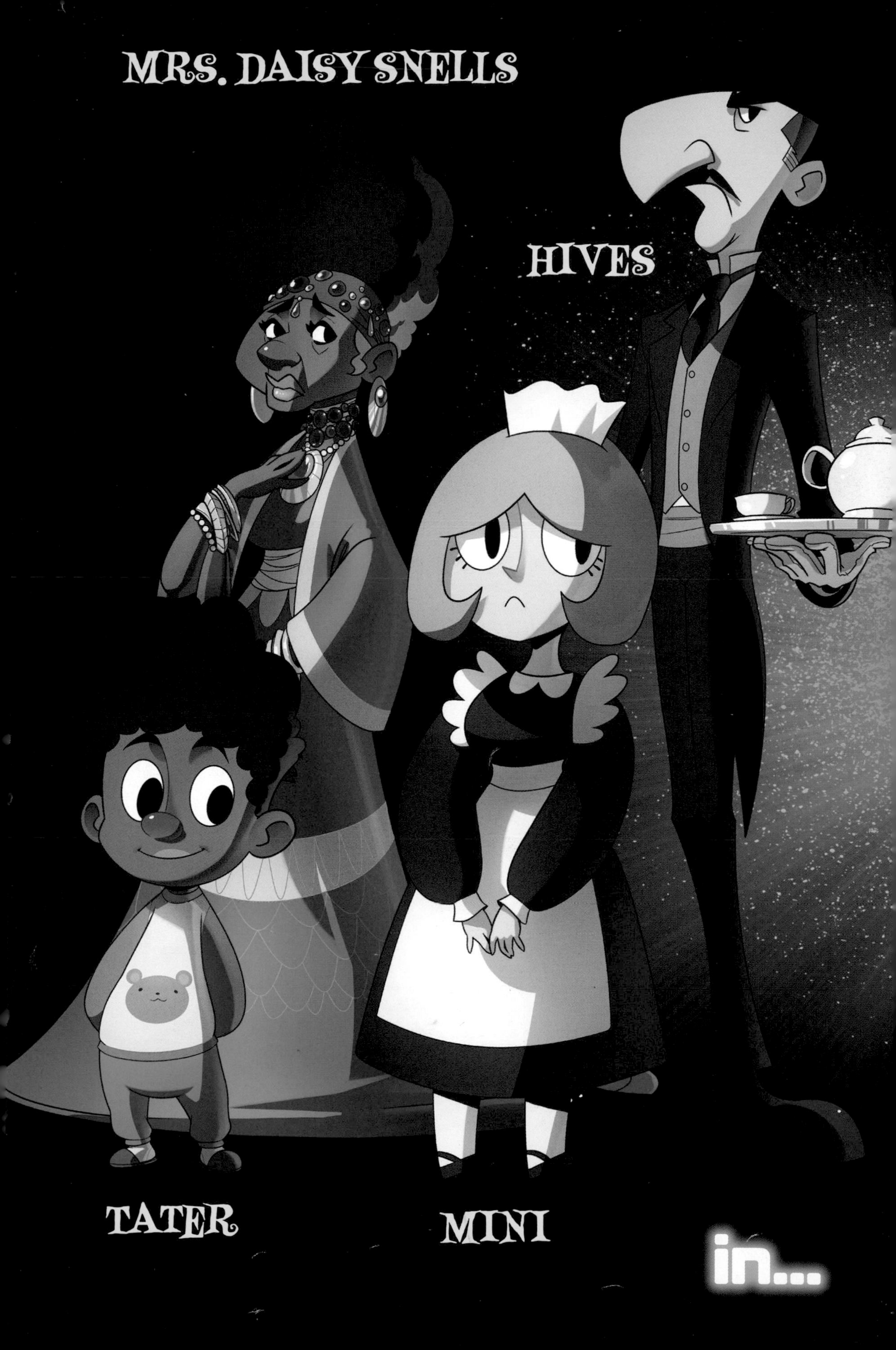
MRS. DAISY SNELLS
HIVES
TATER
MINI
in...

Far Out Fairy Tales is published by
Stone Arch Books
a Capstone imprint
1710 Roe Crest Drive
North Mankato, Minnesota 56003
www.capstonepub.com

Cataloging-in-Publication Data is
available at the Library of Congress
website.
ISBN: 978-1-4965-8394-9 (hardcover)
ISBN: 978-1-4965-8443-4 (paperback)
ISBN: 978-1-4965-8399-4 (eBook PDF)

Summary: Private Eye Princess King is
taking on her toughest case yet: find
the "pea," a priceless emerald that's
disappeared from Mrs. Snells's jewelry
collection. But as Princess searches for
clues, she discovers that Snells Manor
holds many mysteries. Can Princess use
her skills to solve the crime and prove
she's a real detective?

Designed by Hilary Wacholz
Edited by Abby Huff
Lettered by Jaymes Reed

For my Leia—M.P.

Printed and bound in the USA.
PA70

PRIVATE EYE

PRINCESS

AND THE EMERALD PEA

A GRAPHIC NOVEL

BY MARTIN POWELL

ILLUSTRATED BY FERN CANO

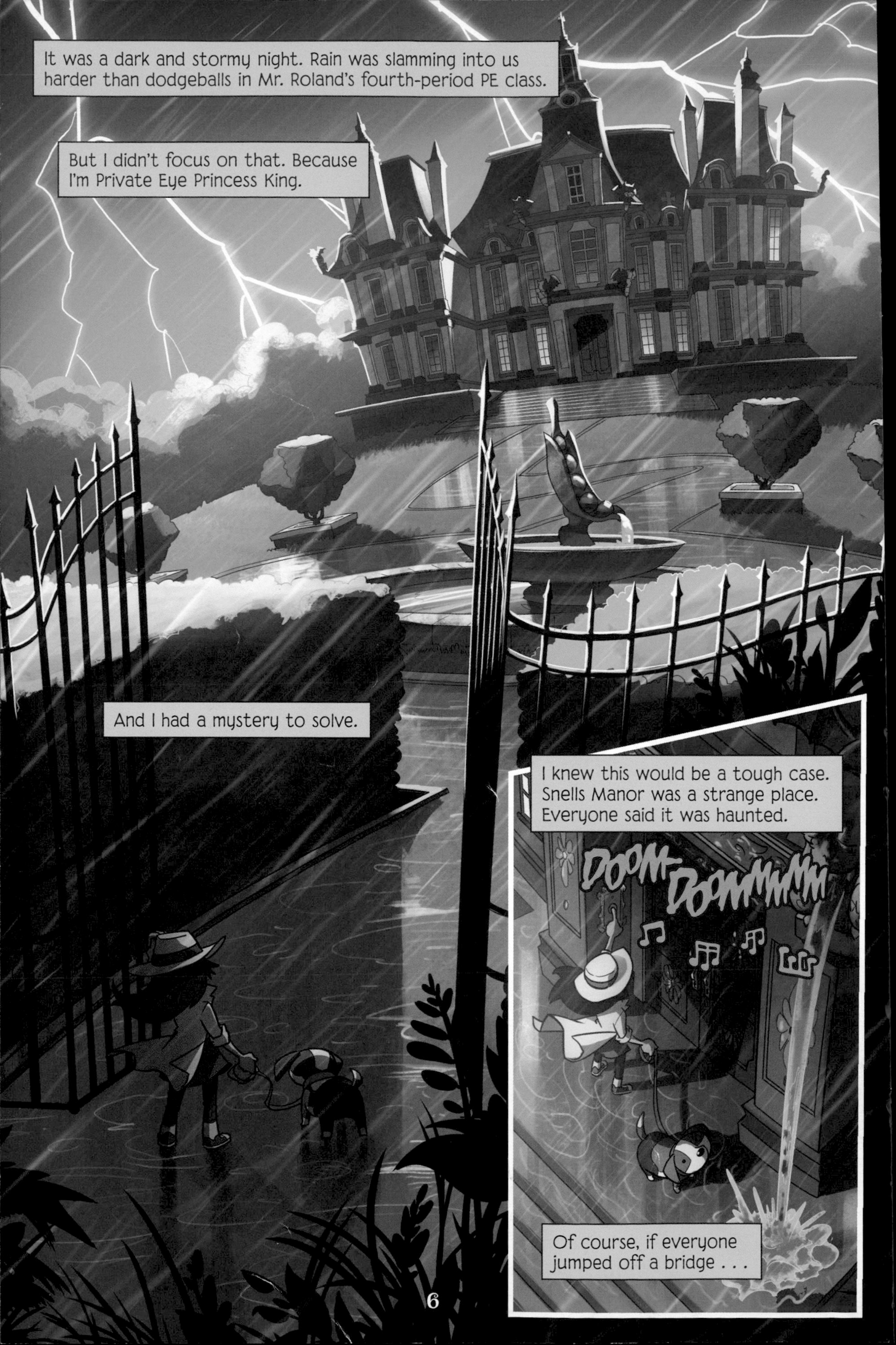
It was a dark and stormy night. Rain was slamming into us harder than dodgeballs in Mr. Roland's fourth-period PE class.
But I didn't focus on that. Because I'm Private Eye Princess King.
And I had a mystery to solve.
I knew this would be a tough case. Snells Manor was a strange place. Everyone said it was haunted.
DOOM-DOOMMMM
Of course, if everyone jumped off a bridge . . .

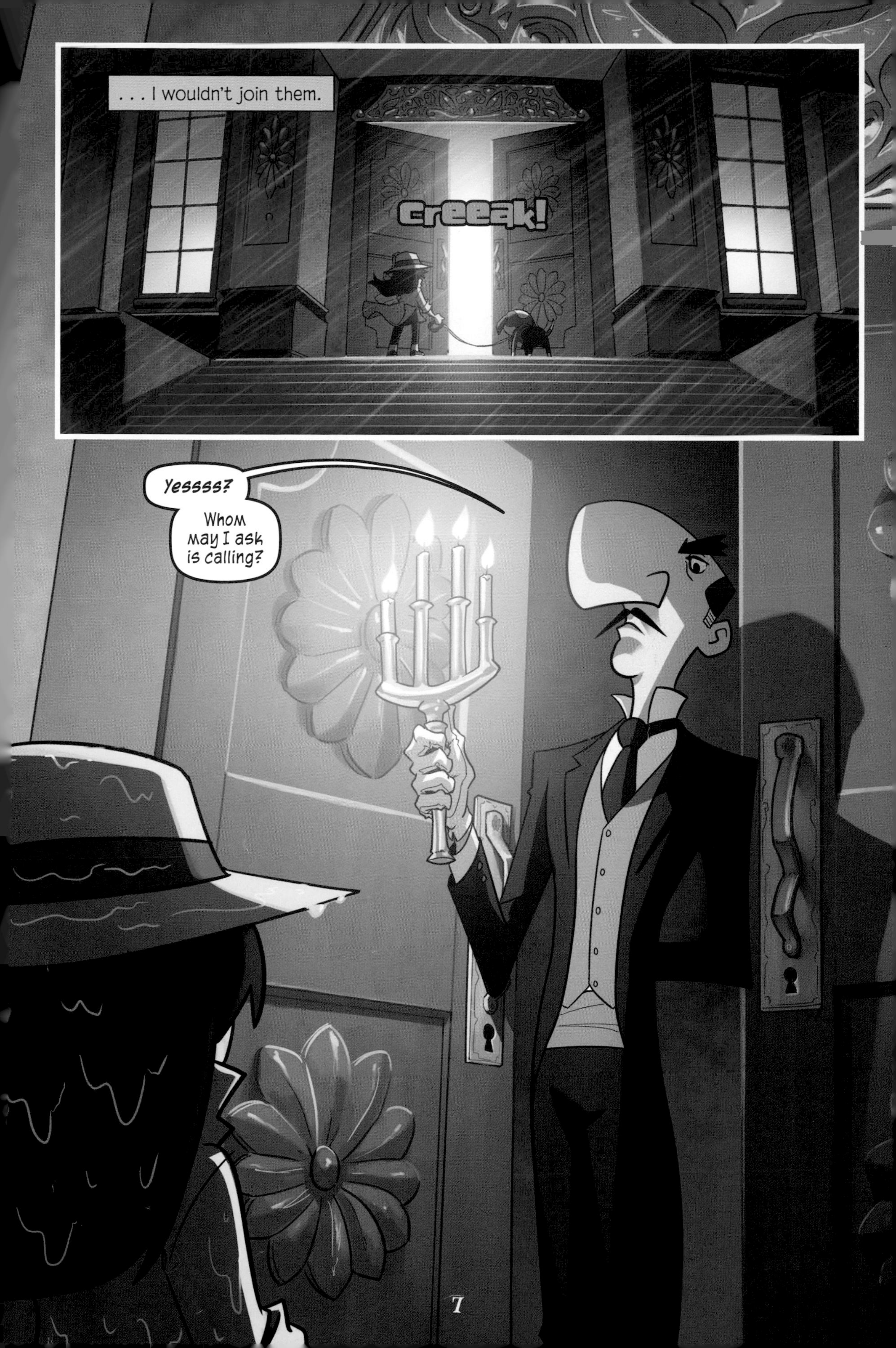
. . . I wouldn't join them.
Creeak!
Yessss?
Whom may I ask is calling?

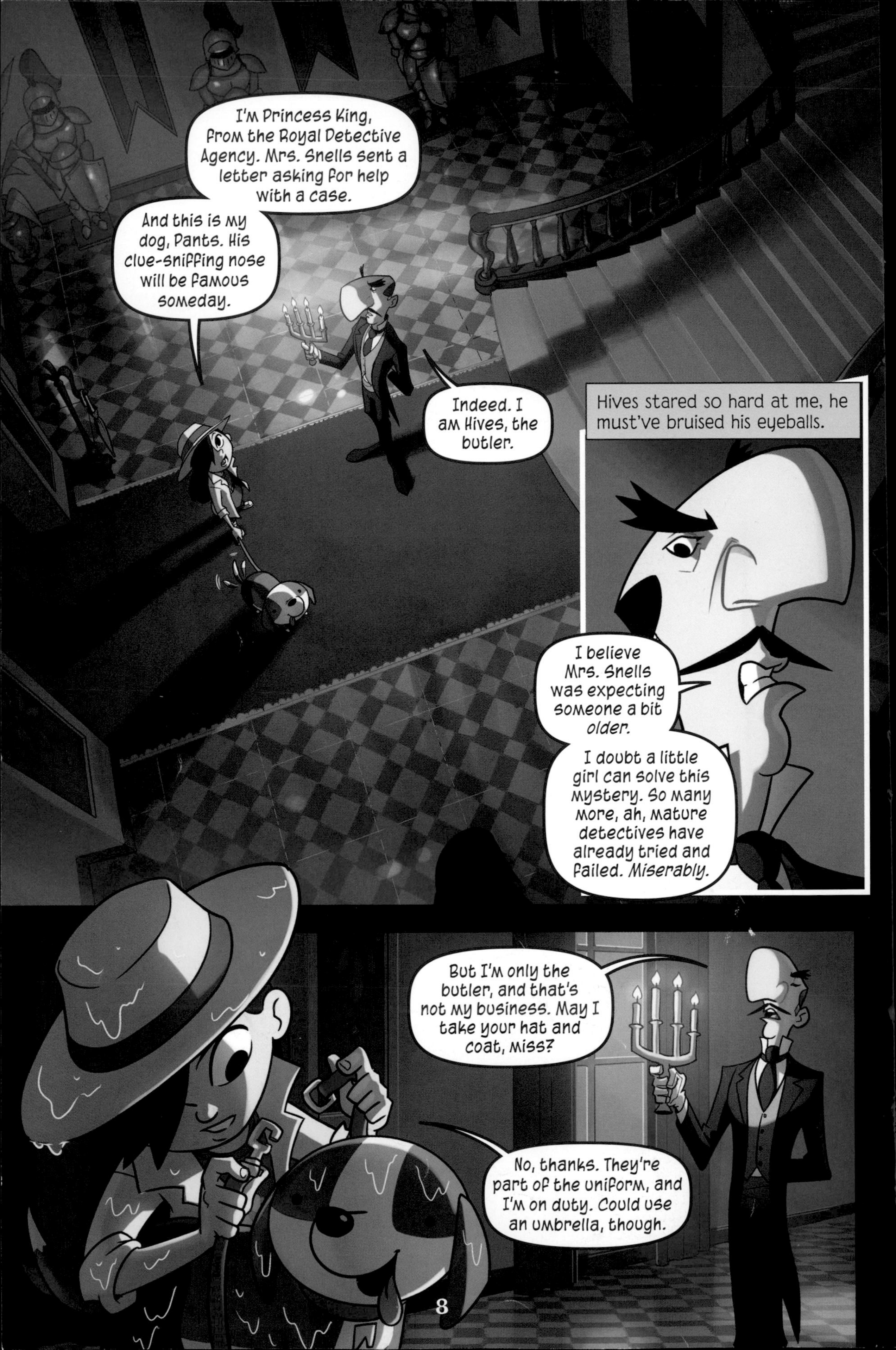
I'm Princess King, from the Royal Detective Agency. Mrs. Snells sent a letter asking for help with a case.
And this is my dog, Pants. His clue-sniffing nose will be famous someday.
Indeed. I am Hives, the butler.
Hives stared so hard at me, he must've bruised his eyeballs.
I believe Mrs. Snells was expecting someone a bit *older.*
I doubt a little girl can solve this mystery. So many more, ah, mature detectives have already tried and failed. *Miserably.*
But I'm only the butler, and that's not my business. May I take your hat and coat, miss?
No, thanks. They're part of the uniform, and I'm on duty. Could use an umbrella, though.

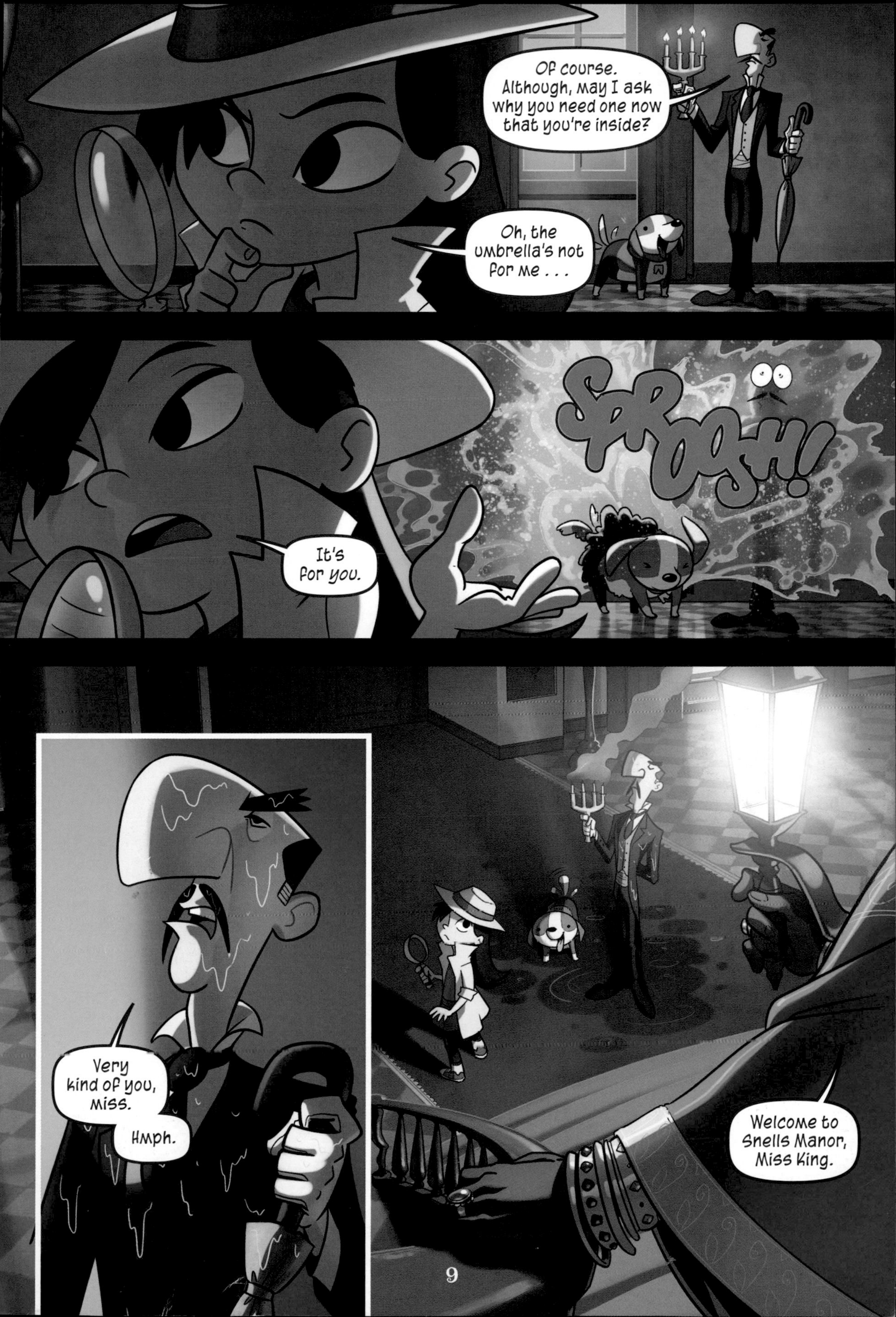
Of course. Although, may I ask why you need one now that you're inside?
Oh, the umbrella's not for me . . .
SPROOSH!!
It's for you.
Very kind of you, Miss.
Hmph.
Welcome to Snells Manor, Miss King.

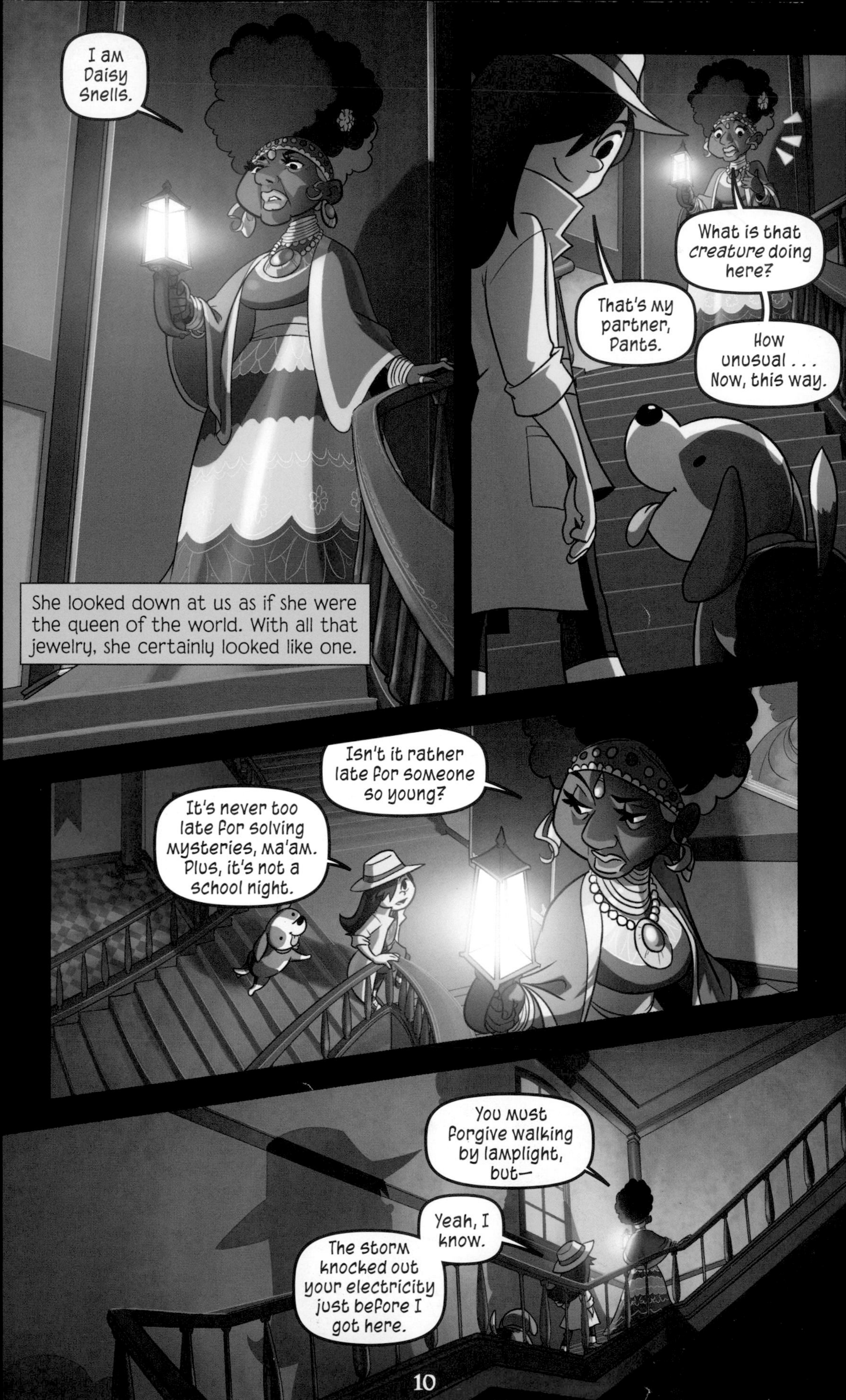
I am Daisy Snells.
She looked down at us as if she were the queen of the world. With all that jewelry, she certainly looked like one.
What is that *creature* doing here?
That's my partner, Pants.
How unusual . . . Now, this way.
Isn't it rather late for someone so young?
It's never too late for solving mysteries, Ma'am. Plus, it's not a school night.
You must forgive walking by lamplight, but—
Yeah, I know.
The storm knocked out your electricity just before I got here.

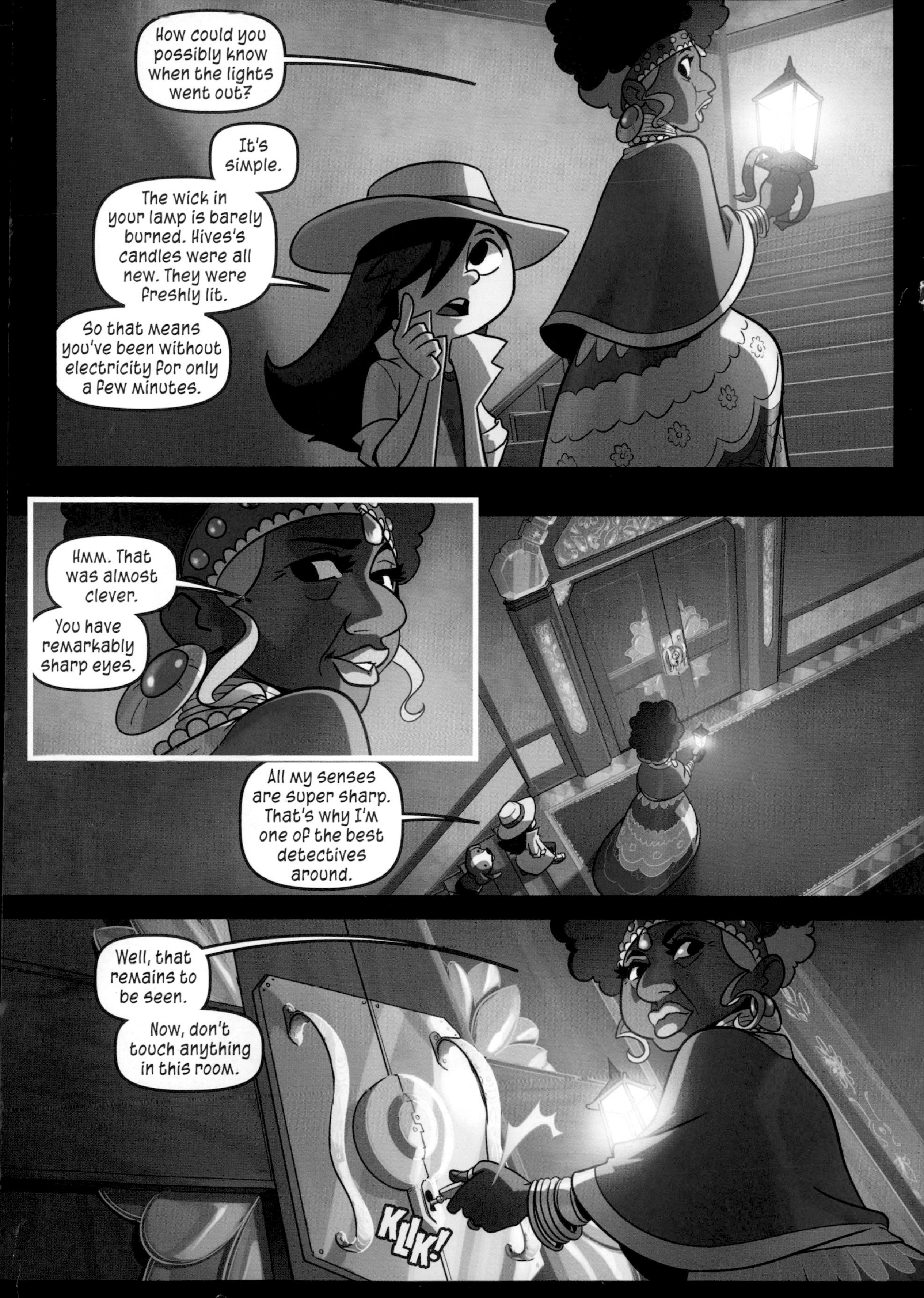
How could you possibly know when the lights went out?
It's simple.
The wick in your lamp is barely burned. Hives's candles were all new. They were freshly lit.
So that means you've been without electricity for only a few minutes.
Hmm. That was almost clever.
You have remarkably sharp eyes.
All my senses are super sharp. That's why I'm one of the best detectives around.
Well, that remains to be seen.
Now, don't touch anything in this room.
KLIK!

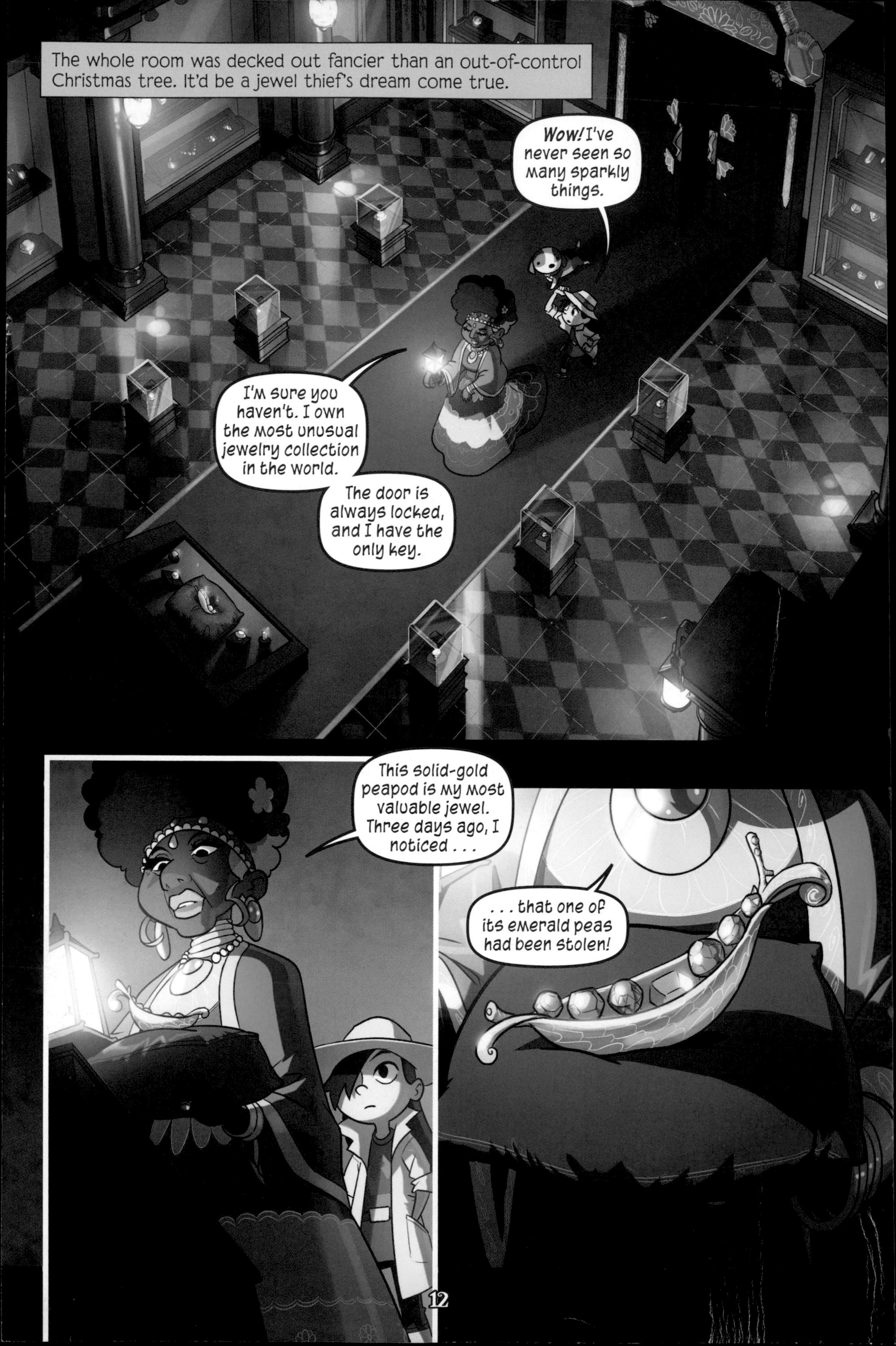
The whole room was decked out fancier than an out-of-control Christmas tree. It'd be a jewel thief's dream come true.
Wow! I've never seen so many sparkly things.
I'm sure you haven't. I own the most unusual jewelry collection in the world.
The door is always locked, and I have the only key.
This solid-gold peapod is my most valuable jewel. Three days ago, I noticed . . .
. . . that one of its emerald peas had been stolen!

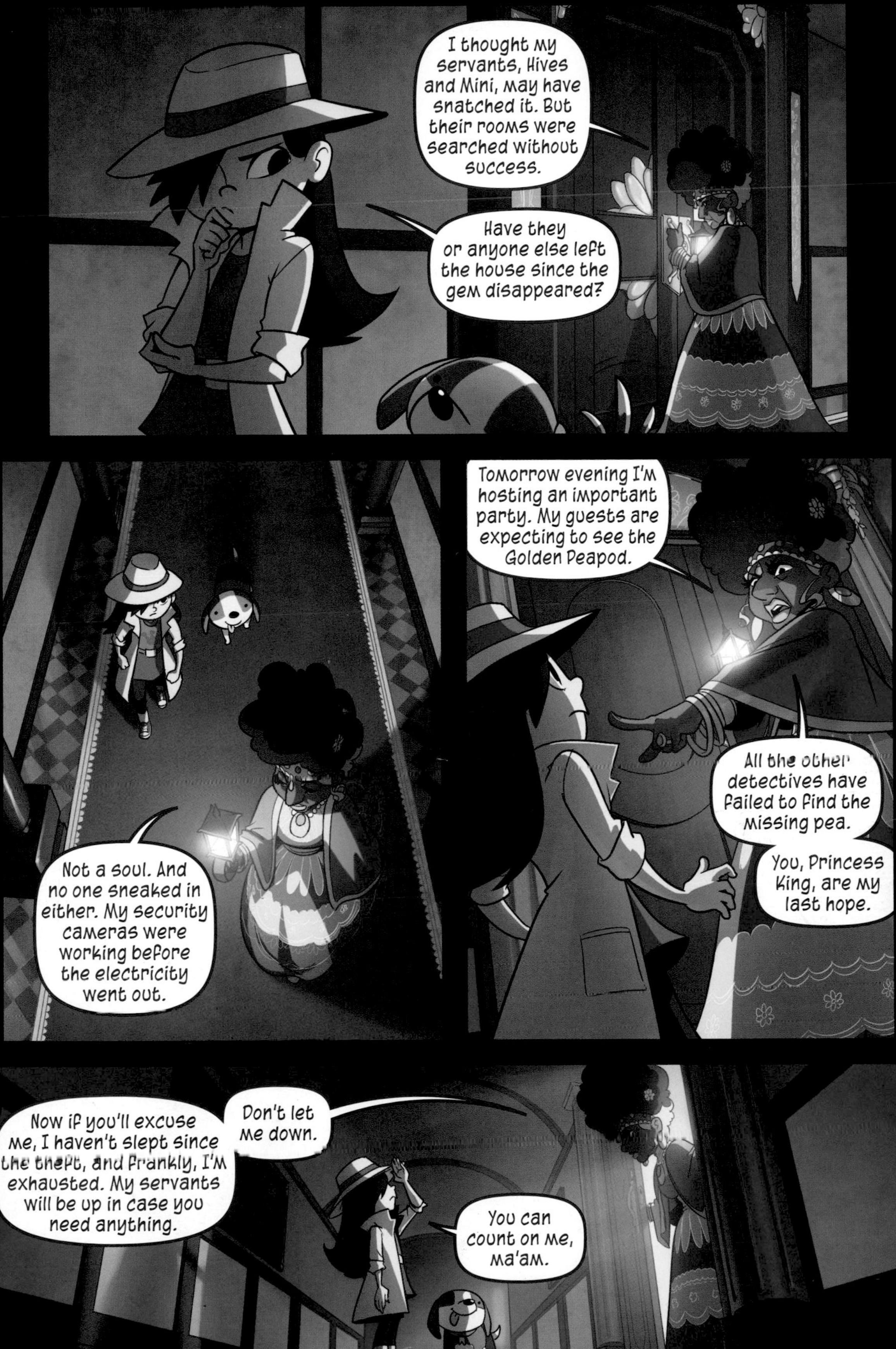
I thought my servants, Hives and Mini, may have snatched it. But their rooms were searched without success.
Have they or anyone else left the house since the gem disappeared?
Not a soul. And no one sneaked in either. My security cameras were working before the electricity went out.
Tomorrow evening I'm hosting an important party. My guests are expecting to see the Golden Peapod.
All the other detectives have failed to find the missing pea.
You, Princess King, are my last hope.
Now if you'll excuse me, I haven't slept since the theft, and frankly, I'm exhausted. My servants will be up in case you need anything.
Don't let me down.
You can count on me, ma'am.

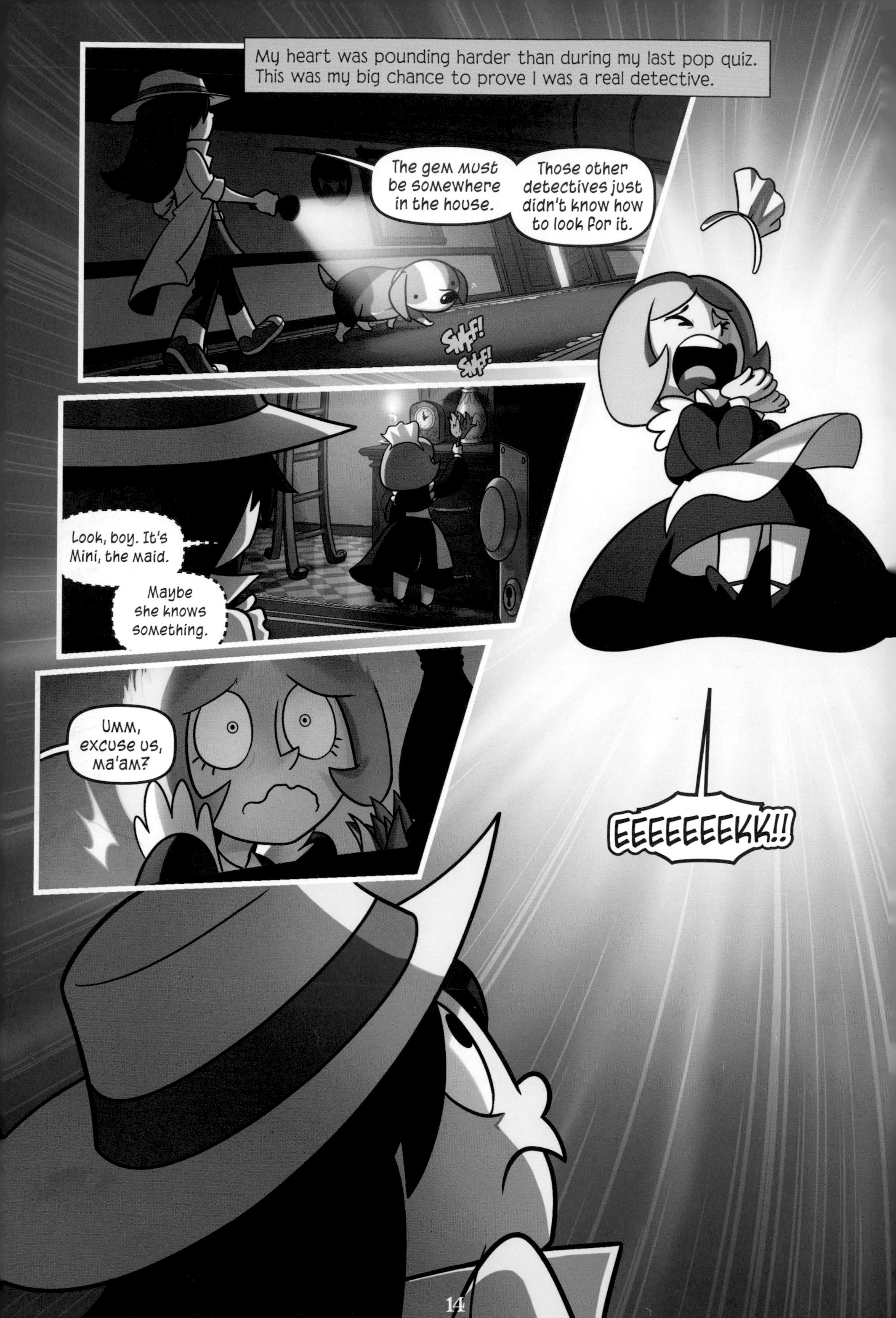
My heart was pounding harder than during my last pop quiz. This was my big chance to prove I was a real detective.
The gem must be somewhere in the house.
Those other detectives just didn't know how to look for it.
SNIFF! SNIFF!
Look, boy. It's Mini, the maid.
Maybe she knows something.
Umm, excuse us, ma'am?
EEEEEEEEKK!!

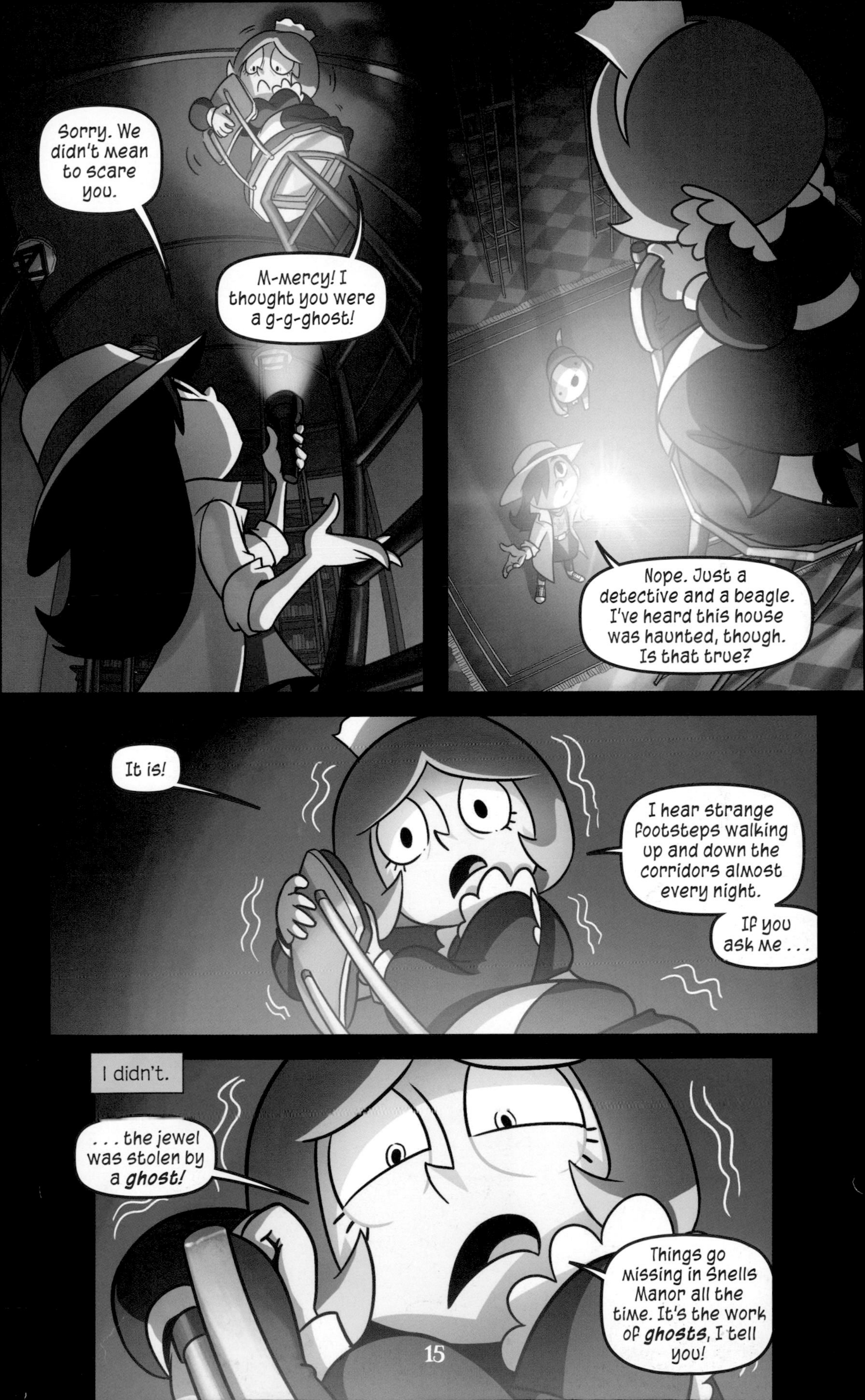
Sorry. We didn't mean to scare you.
M-mercy! I thought you were a g-g-ghost!
Nope. Just a detective and a beagle. I've heard this house was haunted, though. Is that true?
It is!
I hear strange footsteps walking up and down the corridors almost every night.
If you ask me . . .
I didn't.
. . . the jewel was stolen by a ghost!
Things go missing in Snells Manor all the time. It's the work of ghosts, I tell you!

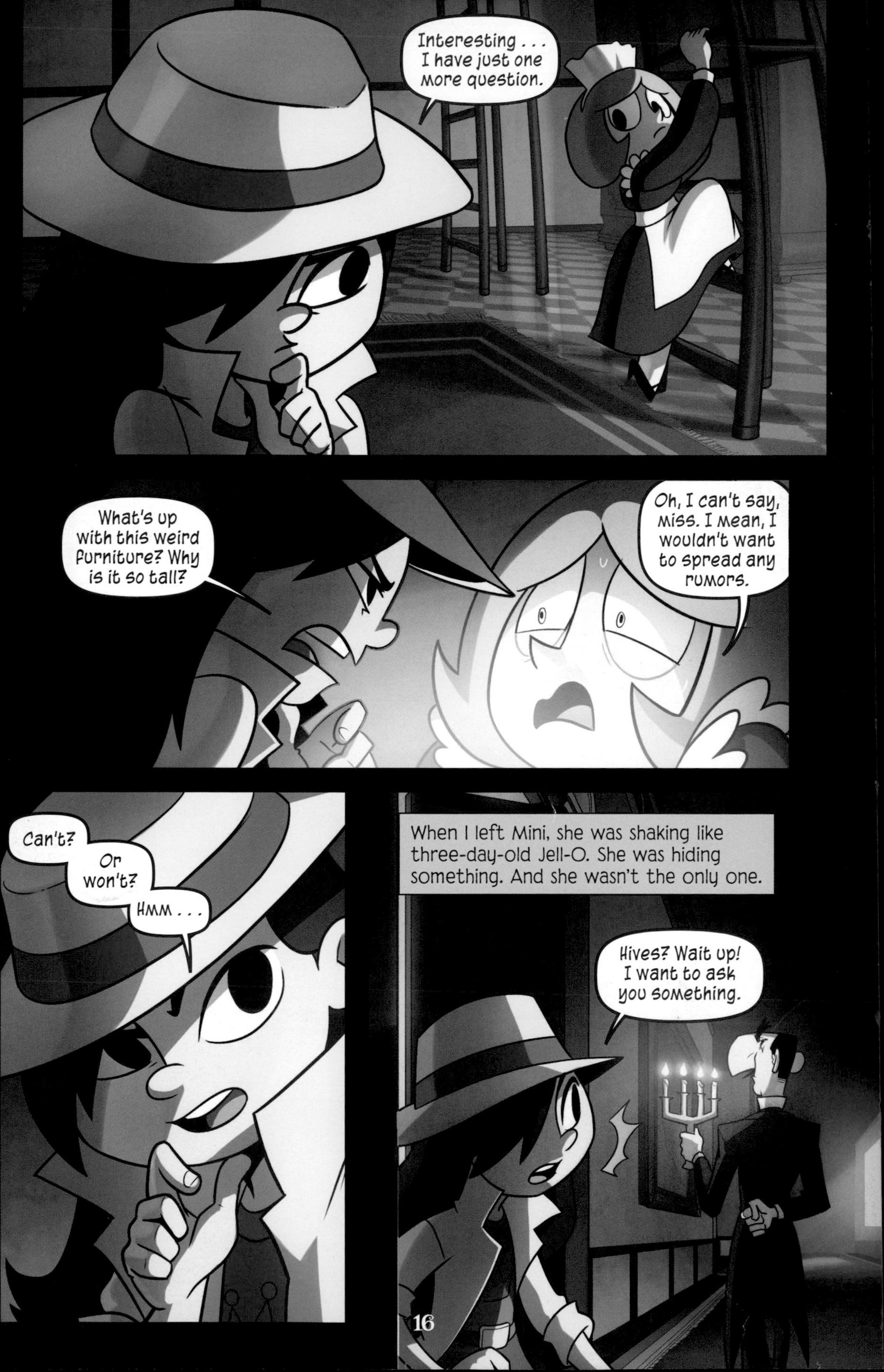
Interesting . . . I have just one more question.
What's up with this weird furniture? Why is it so tall?
Oh, I can't say, miss. I mean, I wouldn't want to spread any rumors.
Can't?
Or won't?
HMM . . .
When I left Mini, she was shaking like three-day-old Jell-O. She was hiding something. And she wasn't the only one.
Hives? Wait up! I want to ask you something.

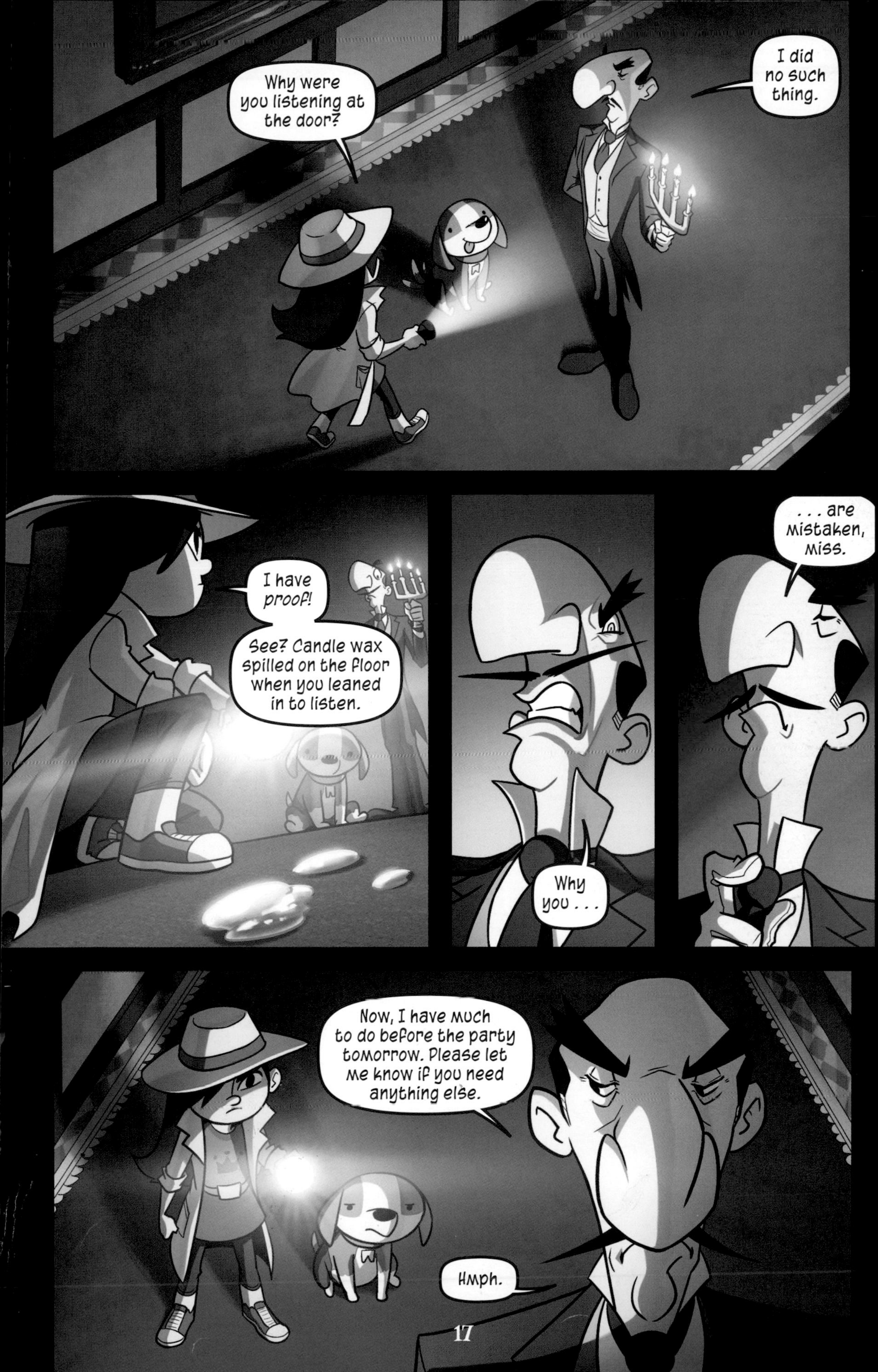

Why were you listening at the door?
I did no such thing.
I have proof!
See? Candle wax spilled on the floor when you leaned in to listen.
Why you . . .
. . . are mistaken, miss.
Now, I have much to do before the party tomorrow. Please let me know if you need anything else.
Hmph.

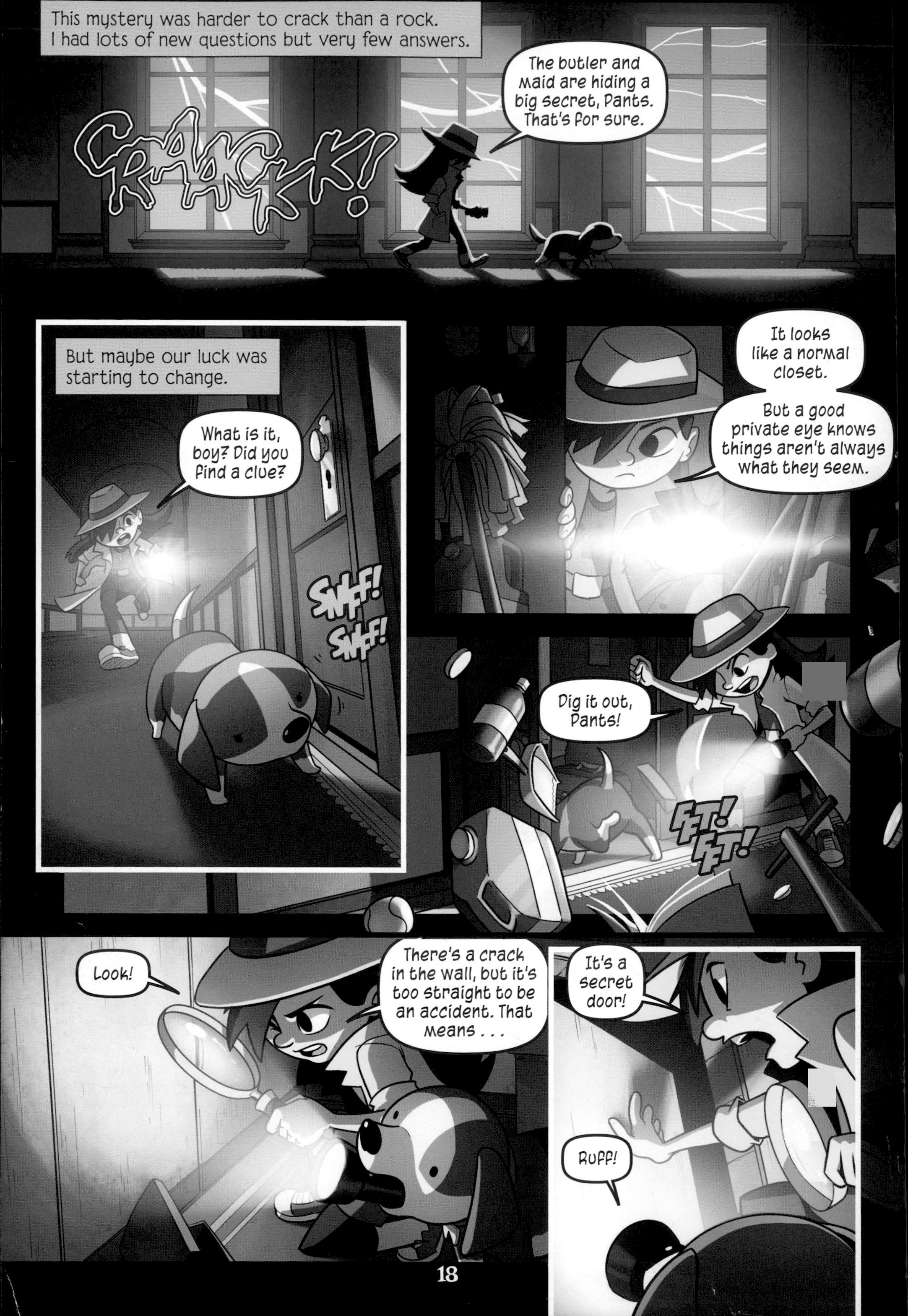

This mystery was harder to crack than a rock.
I had lots of new questions but very few answers.
CRAAACKK!
The butler and maid are hiding a big secret, Pants. That's for sure.
But maybe our luck was starting to change.
What is it, boy? Did you find a clue?
SNIFF! SNIFF!
It looks like a normal closet.
But a good private eye knows things aren't always what they seem.
Dig it out, Pants!
FFT! FFT!
Look!
There's a crack in the wall, but it's too straight to be an accident. That means . . .
It's a secret door!
Ruff!

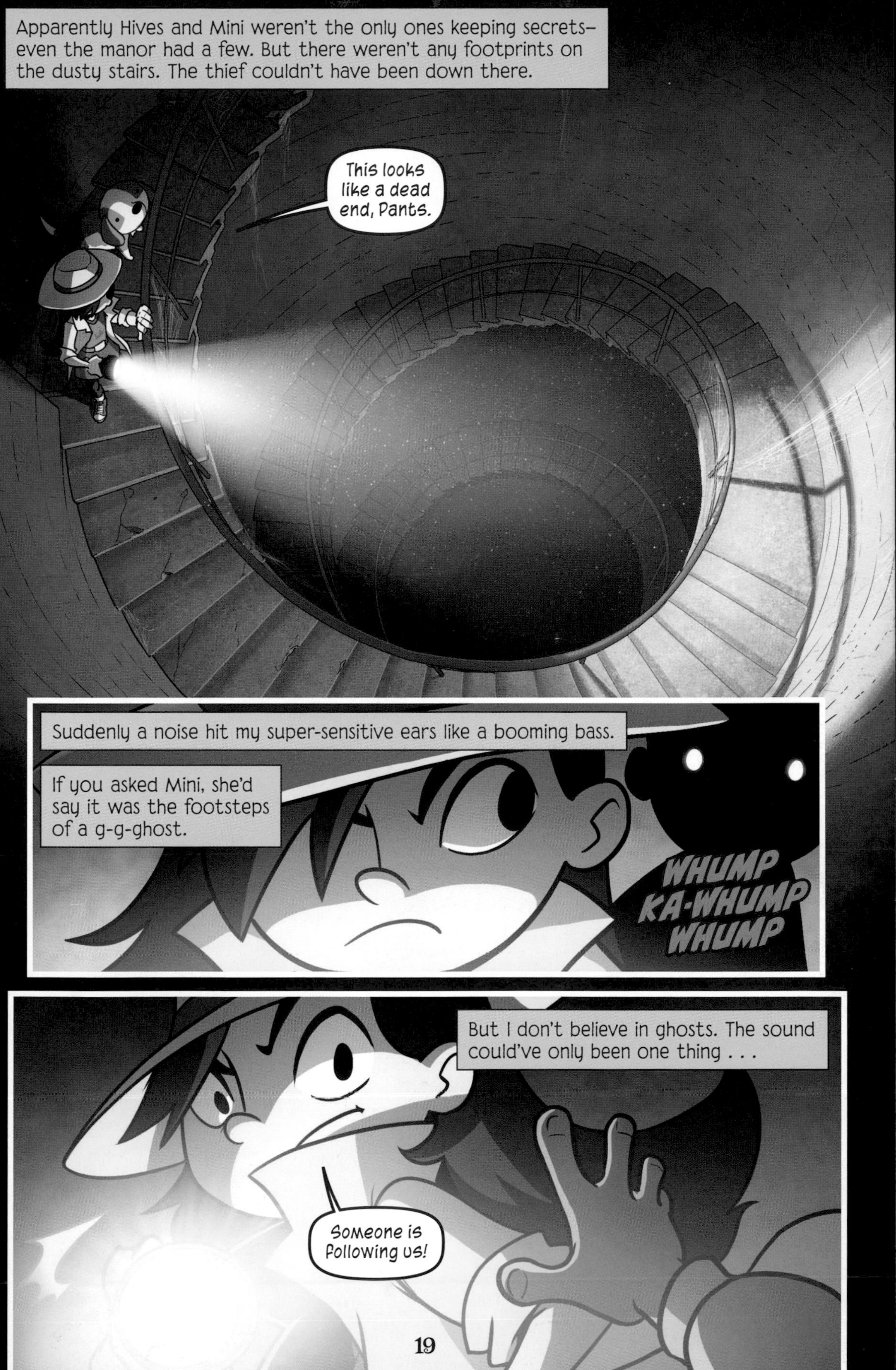

Apparently Hives and Mini weren't the only ones keeping secrets—even the manor had a few. But there weren't any footprints on the dusty stairs. The thief couldn't have been down there.
This looks like a dead end, Pants.
Suddenly a noise hit my super-sensitive ears like a booming bass.
If you asked Mini, she'd say it was the footsteps of a g-g-ghost.
WHUMP KA-WHUMP WHUMP
But I don't believe in ghosts. The sound could've only been one thing . . .
Someone is following us!

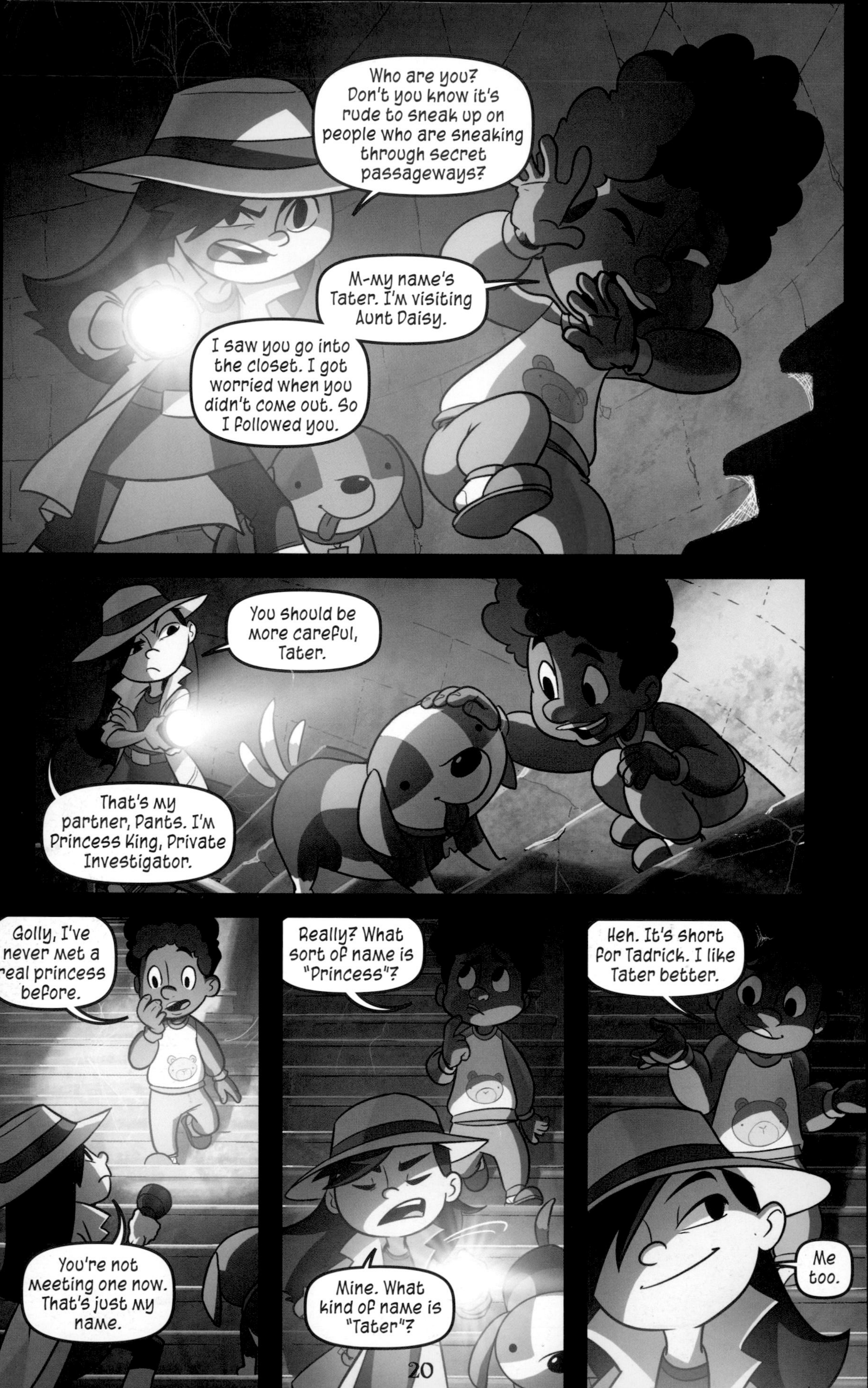
Who are you? Don't you know it's rude to sneak up on people who are sneaking through secret passageways?
M-my name's Tater. I'm visiting Aunt Daisy.
I saw you go into the closet. I got worried when you didn't come out. So I followed you.
You should be more careful, Tater.
That's my partner, Pants. I'm Princess King, Private Investigator.
Golly, I've never met a real princess before.
You're not meeting one now. That's just my name.
Really? What sort of name is "Princess"?
Mine. What kind of name is "Tater"?
Heh. It's short for Tadrick. I like Tater better.
Me too.

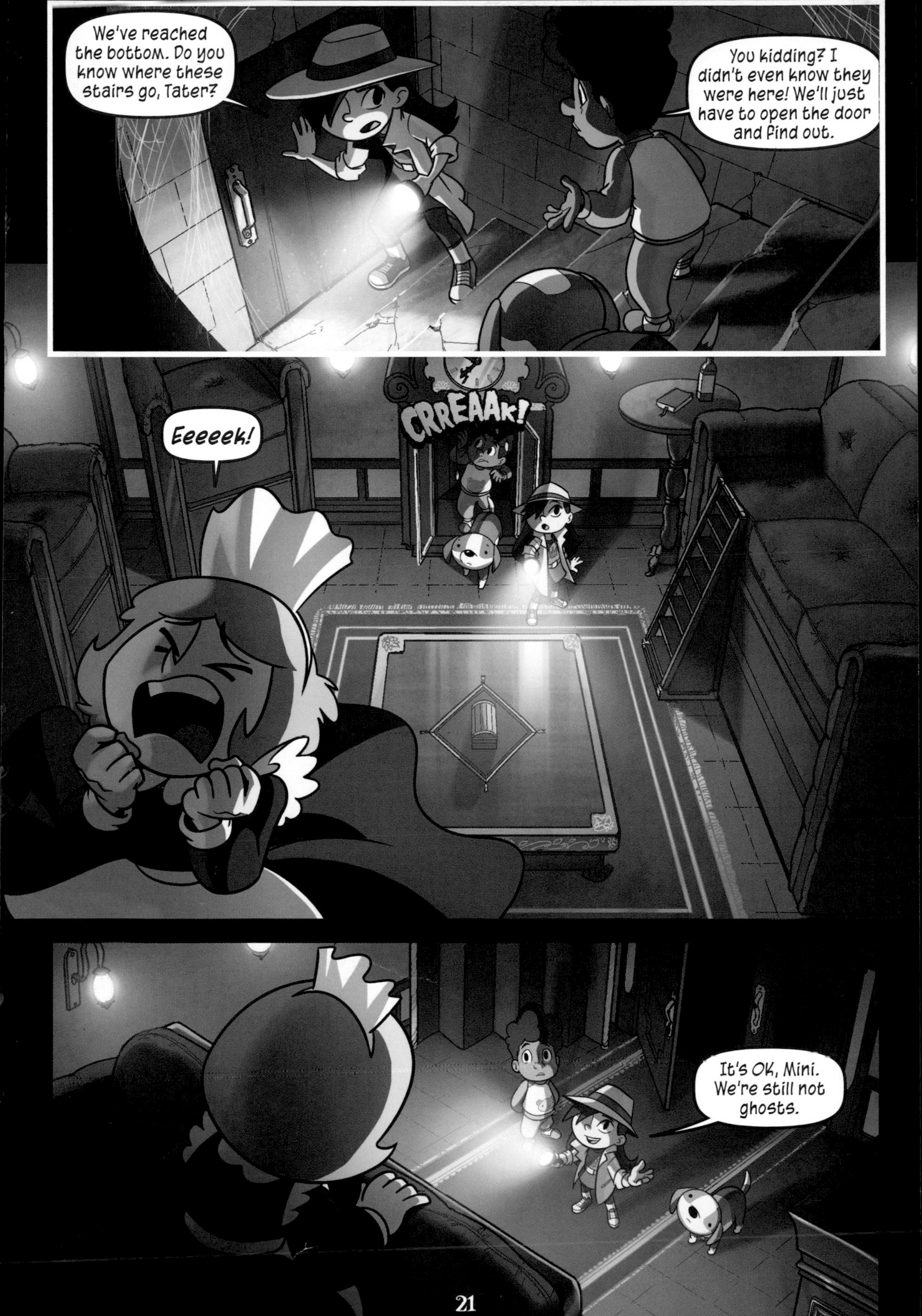
We've reached the bottom. Do you know where these stairs go, Tater?
You kidding? I didn't even know they were here! We'll just have to open the door and find out.
CRREAAK!
Eeeeek!
It's OK, Mini. We're still not ghosts.

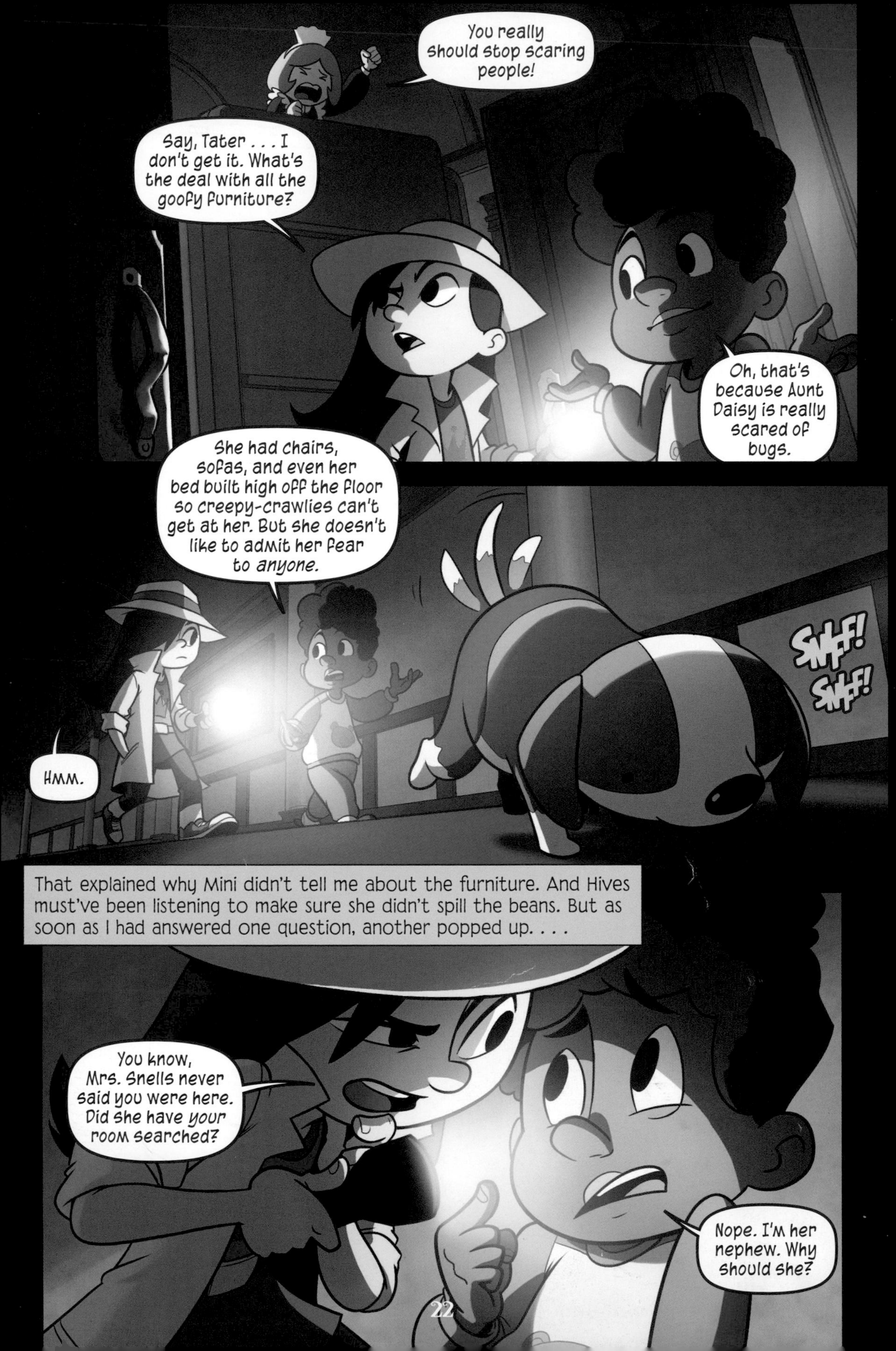
You really should stop scaring people!
Say, Tater . . . I don't get it. What's the deal with all the goofy furniture?
Oh, that's because Aunt Daisy is really scared of bugs.
She had chairs, sofas, and even her bed built high off the floor so creepy-crawlies can't get at her. But she doesn't like to admit her fear to *anyone*.
SNFF! SNFF!
HMM.
That explained why Mini didn't tell me about the furniture. And Hives must've been listening to make sure she didn't spill the beans. But as soon as I had answered one question, another popped up. . . .
You know, Mrs. Snells never said you were here. Did she have *your* room searched?
Nope. I'm her nephew. Why should she?

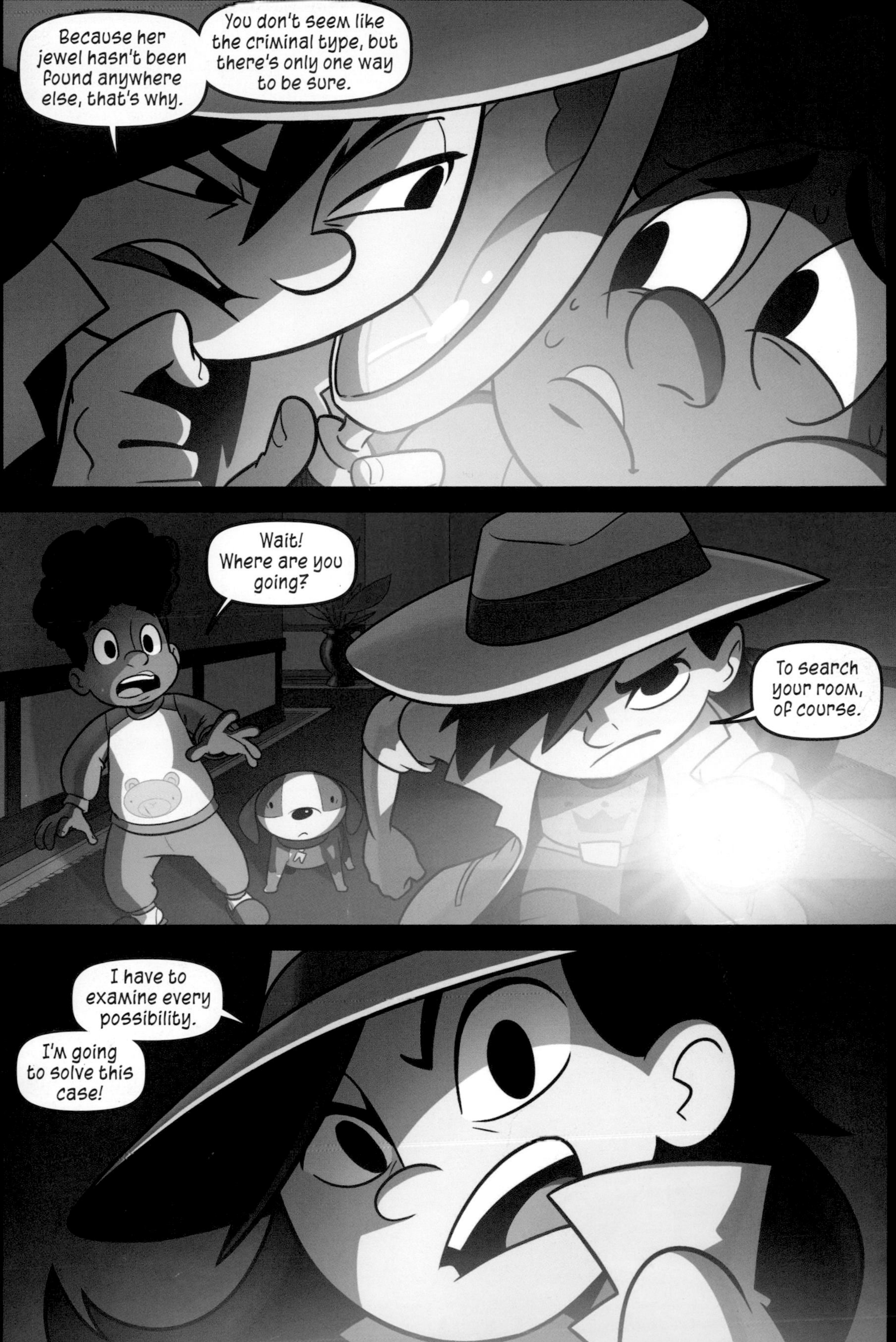
Because her jewel hasn't been found anywhere else, that's why.
You don't seem like the criminal type, but there's only one way to be sure.
Wait! Where are you going?
To search your room, of course.
I have to examine every possibility.
I'm going to solve this case!

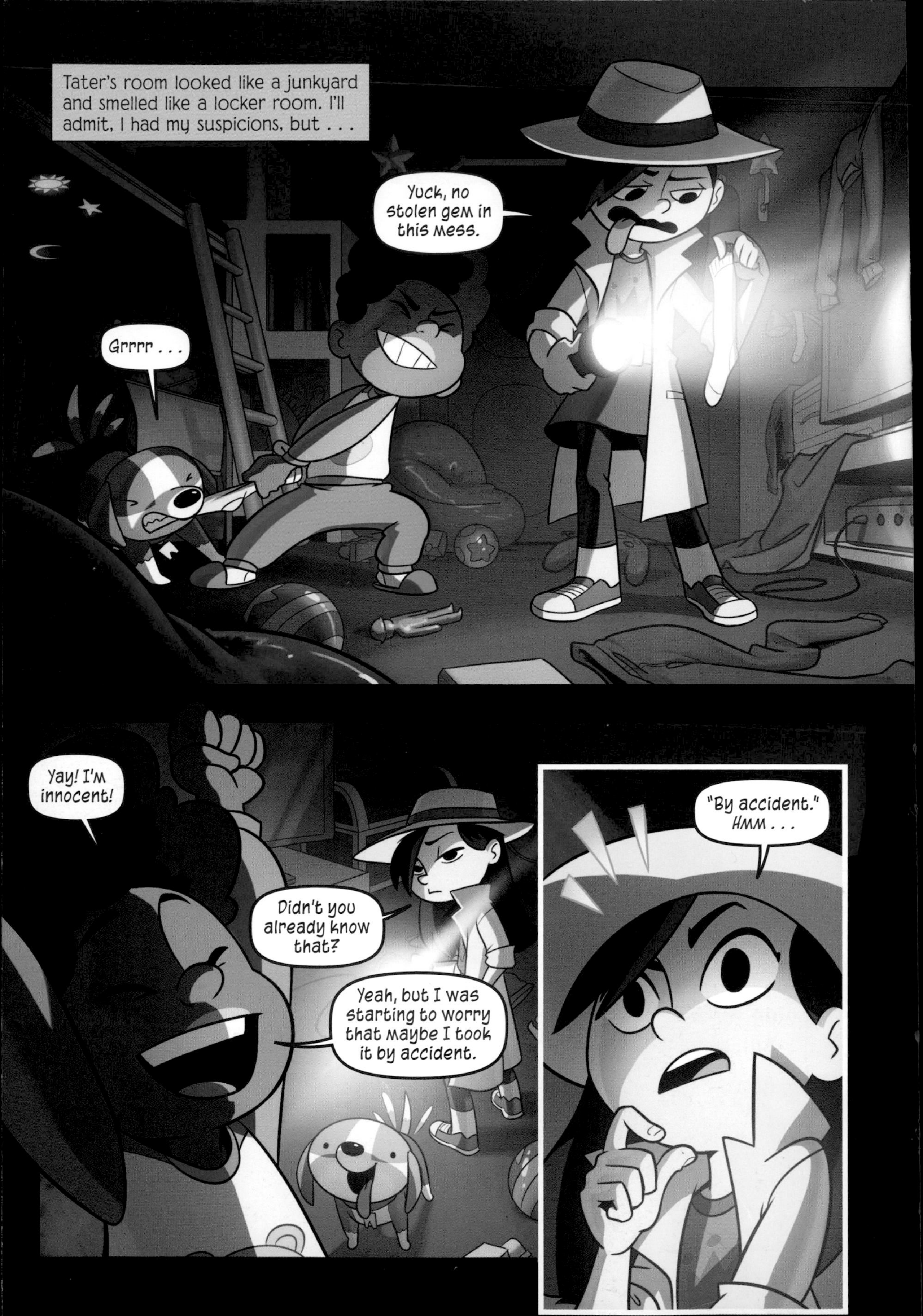
Tater's room looked like a junkyard and smelled like a locker room. I'll admit, I had my suspicions, but . . .
Yuck, no stolen gem in this mess.
Grrrr . . .
Yay! I'm innocent!
Didn't you already know that?
Yeah, but I was starting to worry that maybe I took it by accident.
"By accident." HMM . . .

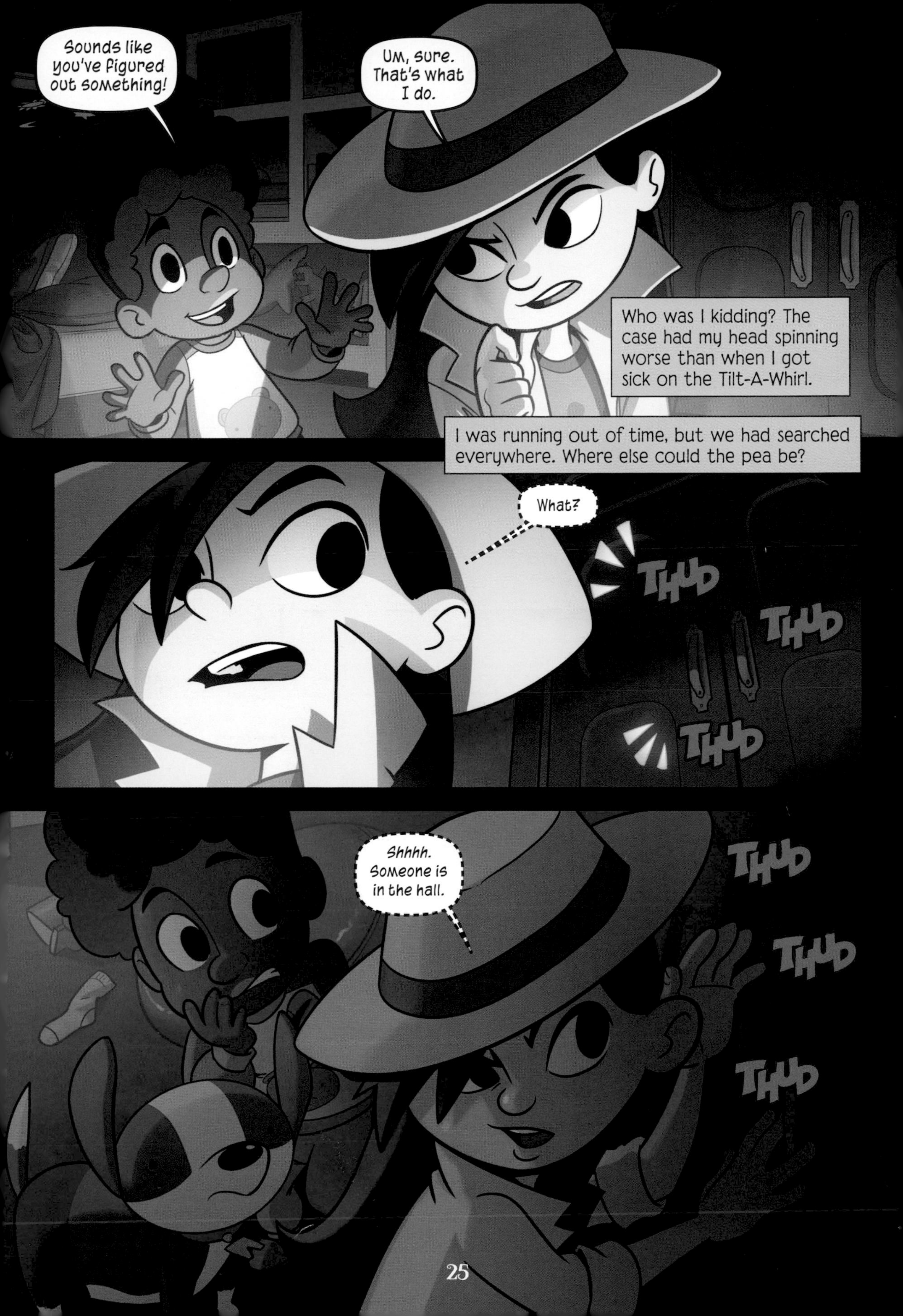
Sounds like you've figured out something!
Um, sure. That's what I do.
Who was I kidding? The case had my head spinning worse than when I got sick on the Tilt-A-Whirl.
I was running out of time, but we had searched everywhere. Where else could the pea be?
What?
THUD
THUD
THUD
Shhhh. Someone is in the hall.
THUD
THUD
THUD

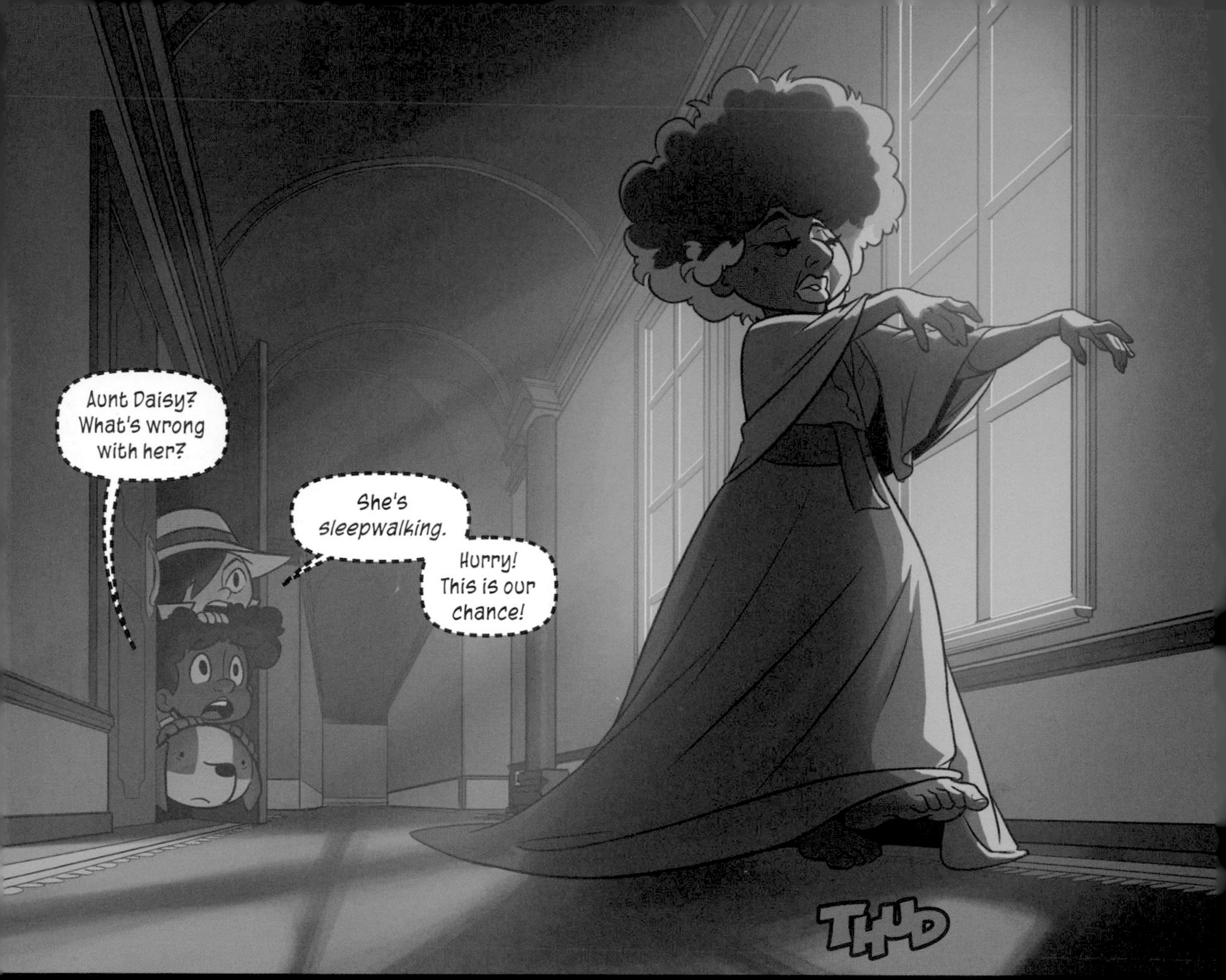
Aunt Daisy? What's wrong with her?
She's sleepwalking.
Hurry! This is our chance!
THUD

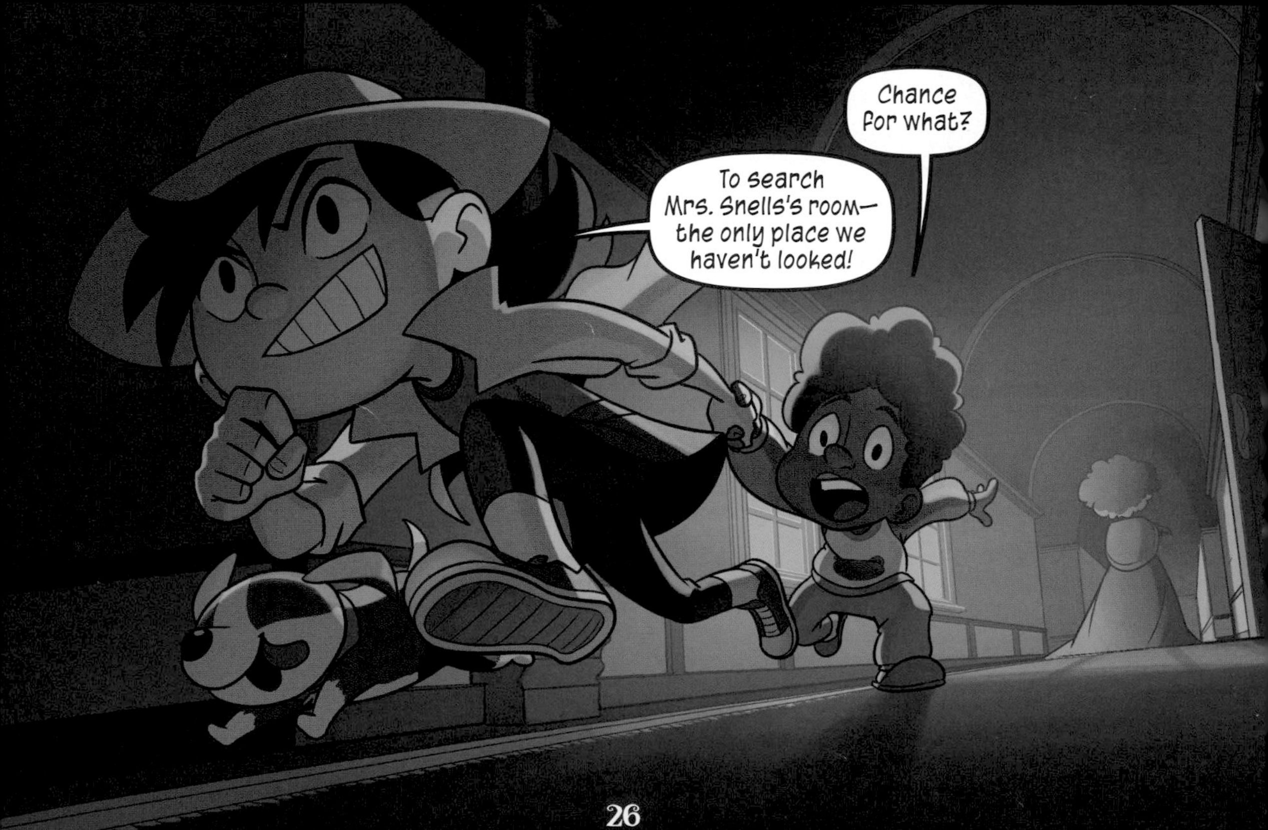
Chance for what?
To search Mrs. Snells's room— the only place we haven't looked!

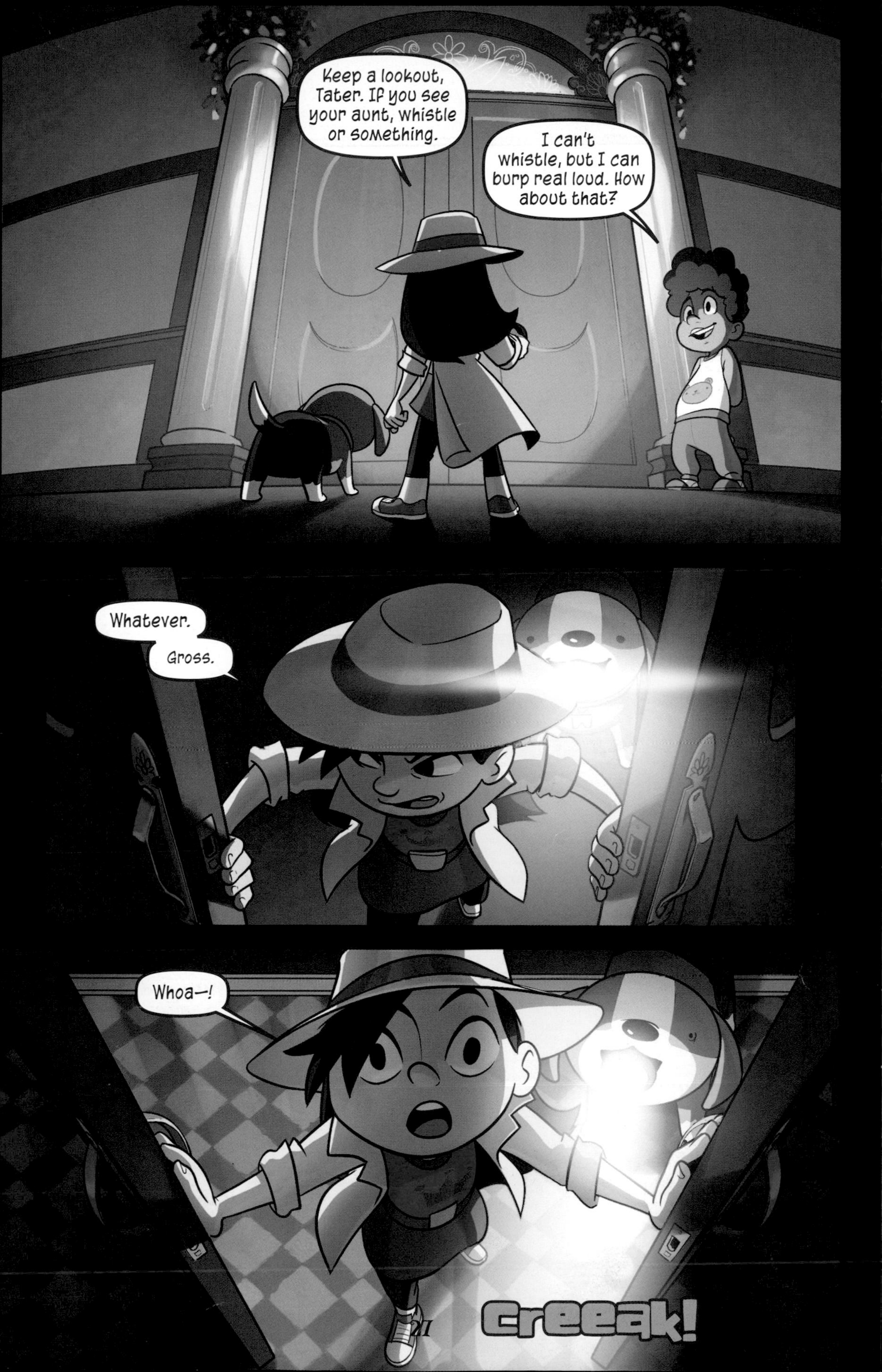
Keep a lookout, Tater. If you see your aunt, whistle or something.
I can't whistle, but I can burp real loud. How about that?
Whatever.
Gross.
Whoa—!
Creeak!

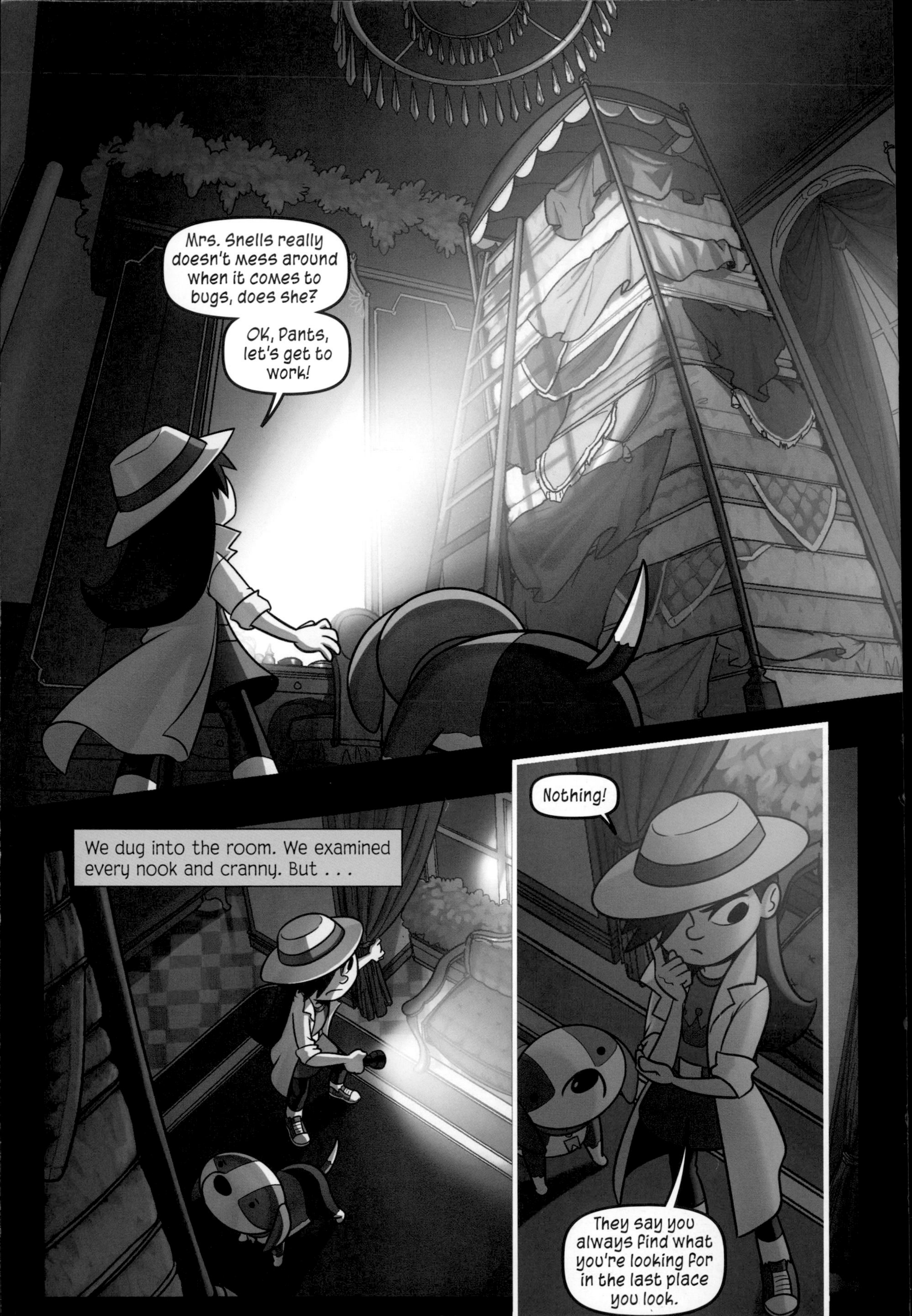

Mrs. Snells really doesn't mess around when it comes to bugs, does she?
OK, Pants, let's get to work!
We dug into the room. We examined every nook and cranny. But . . .
Nothing!
They say you always find what you're looking for in the last place you look.

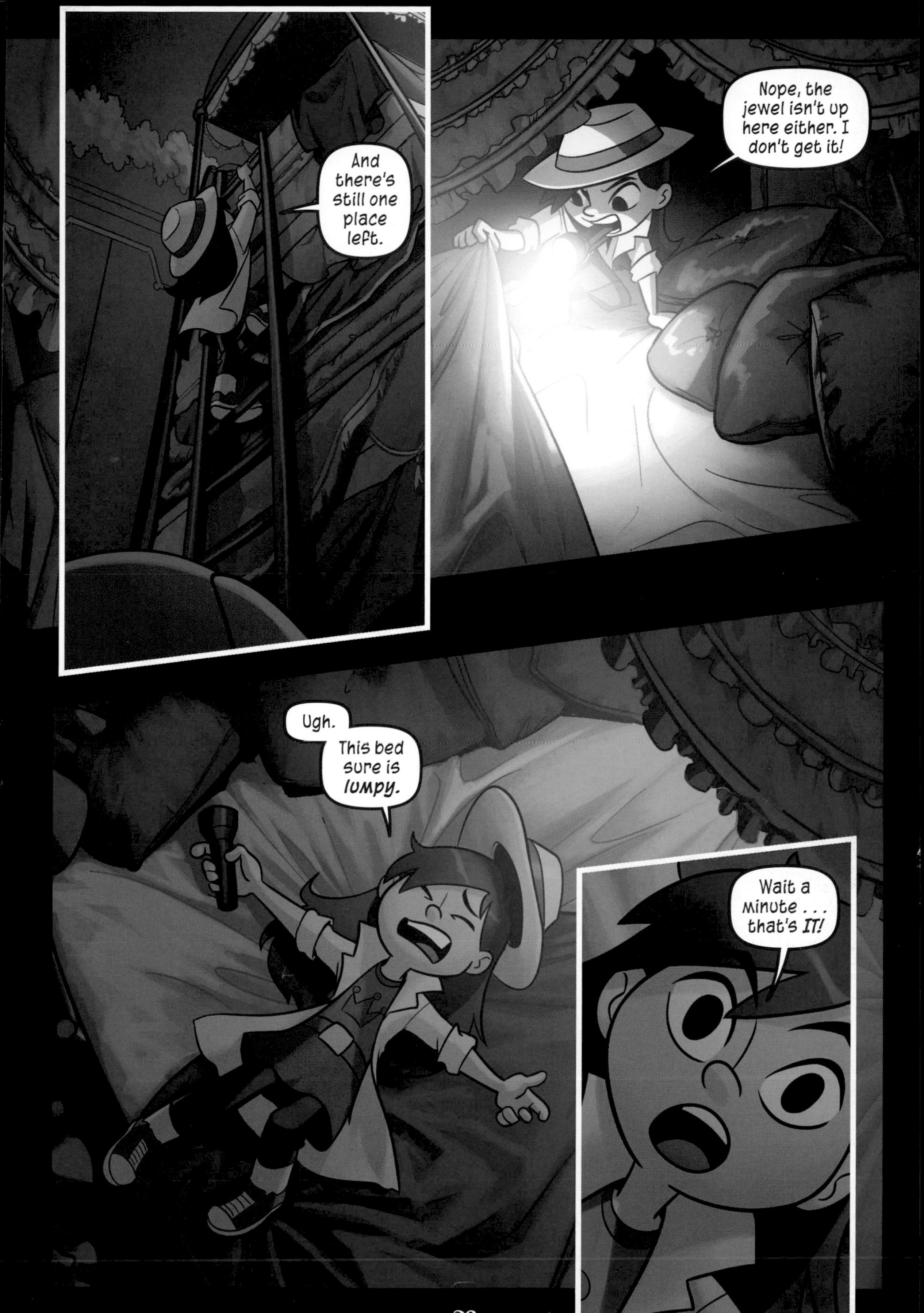
And there's still one place left.
Nope, the jewel isn't up here either. I don't get it!
Ugh.
This bed sure is *lumpy.*
Wait a minute . . . that's *IT!*

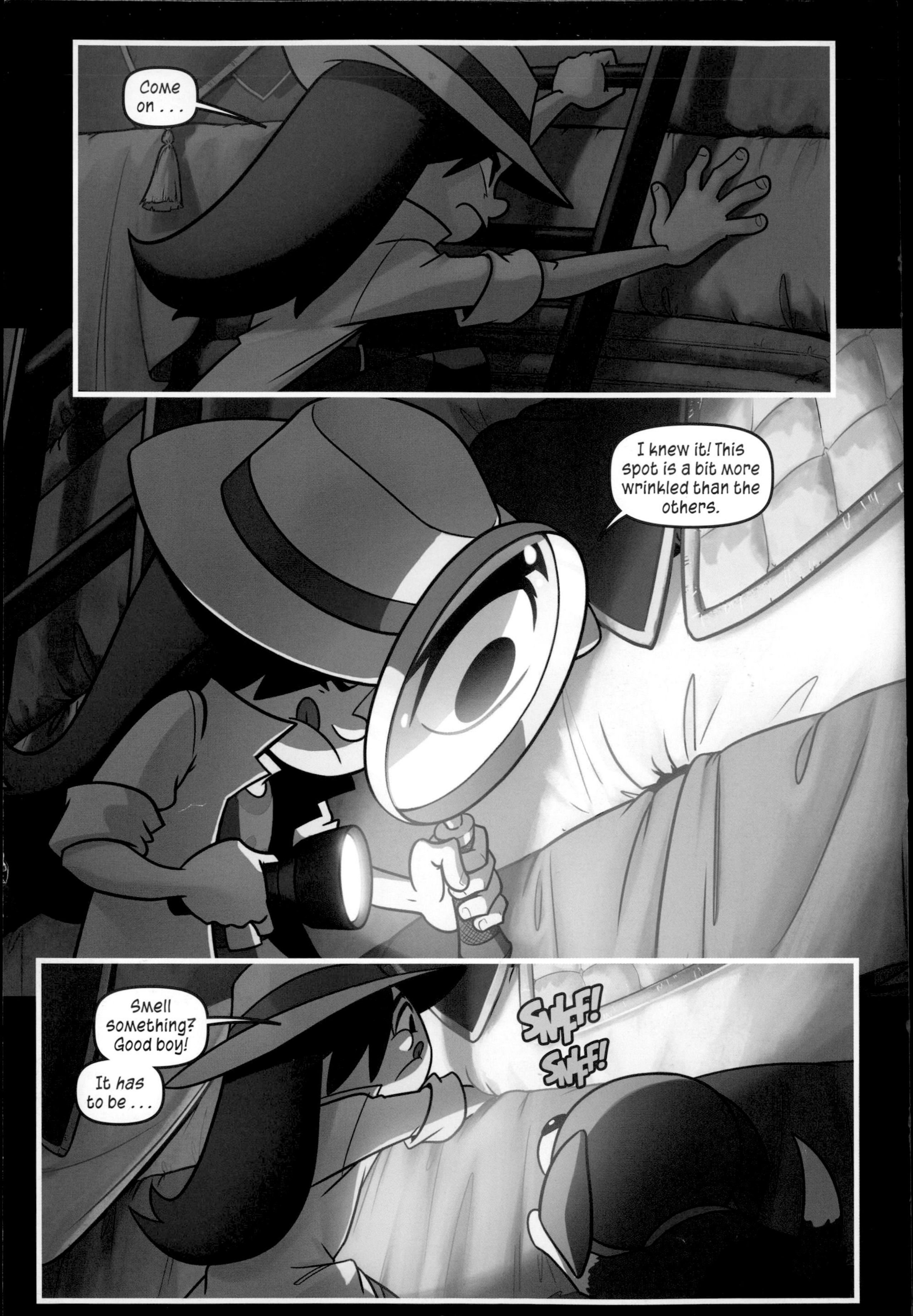
Come on . . .
I knew it! This spot is a bit more wrinkled than the others.
Smell something? Good boy!
It has to be . . .
SNIFF!
SNIFF!

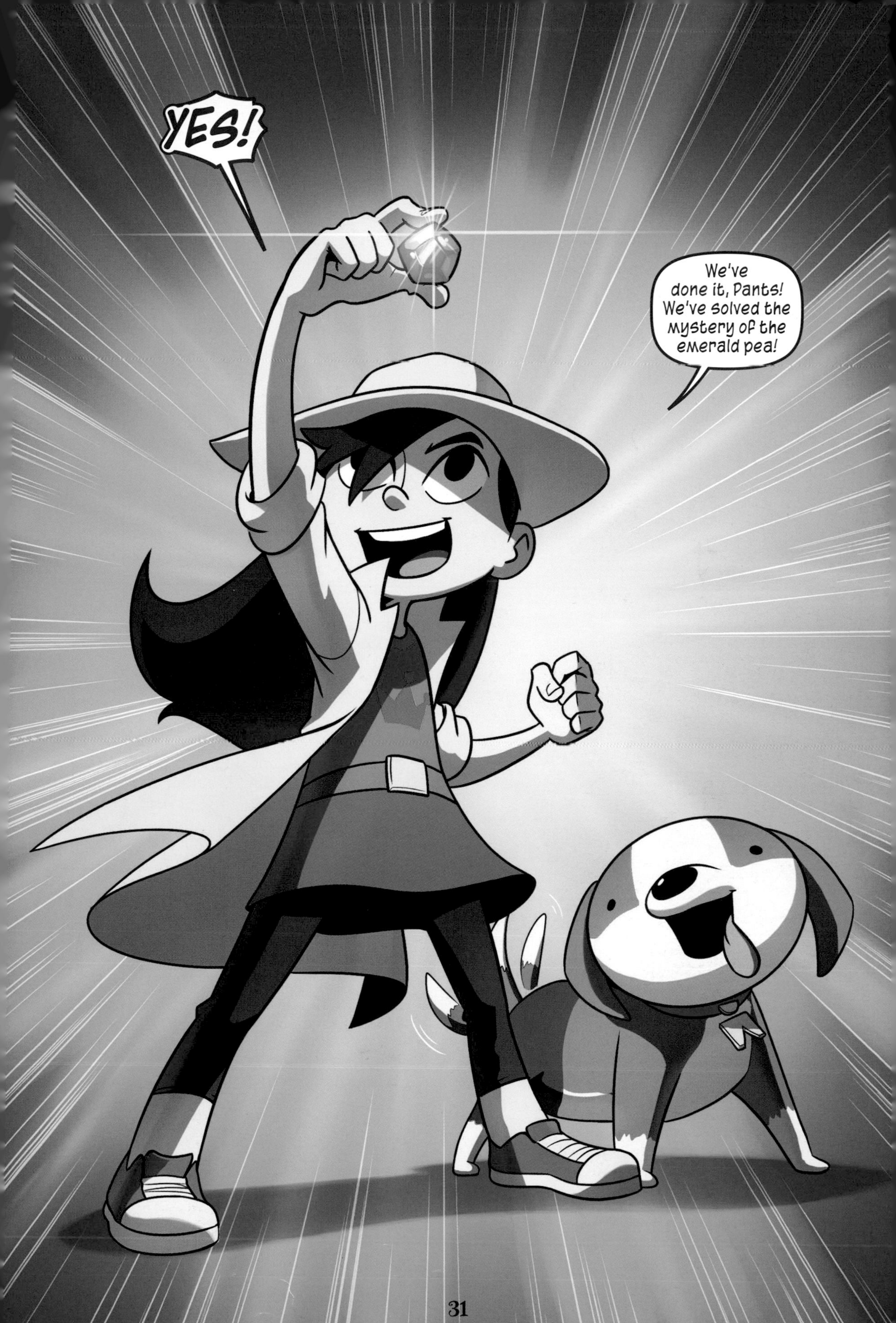
YES!
We've done it, Pants! We've solved the mystery of the emerald pea!

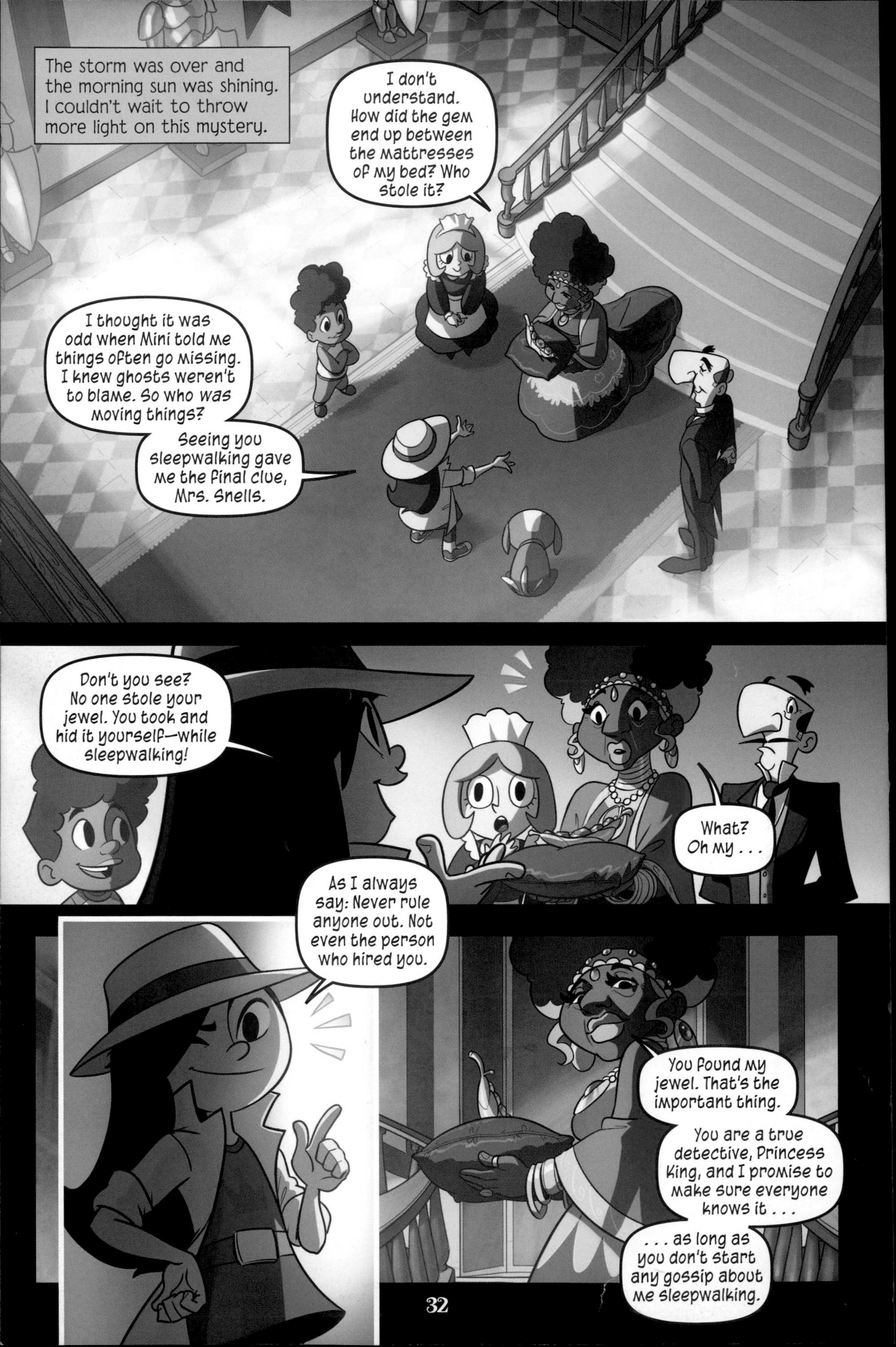
The storm was over and the morning sun was shining. I couldn't wait to throw more light on this mystery.
I don't understand. How did the gem end up between the mattresses of my bed? Who stole it?
I thought it was odd when Mini told me things often go missing. I knew ghosts weren't to blame. So who *was* moving things?
Seeing you sleepwalking gave me the final clue, Mrs. Snells.
Don't you see? No one stole your jewel. You took and hid it yourself—while sleepwalking!
What? Oh my . . .
As I always say: Never rule anyone out. Not even the person who hired you.
You found my jewel. That's the important thing.
You are a true detective, Princess King, and I promise to make sure everyone knows it . . .
. . . as long as you don't start any gossip about me sleepwalking.

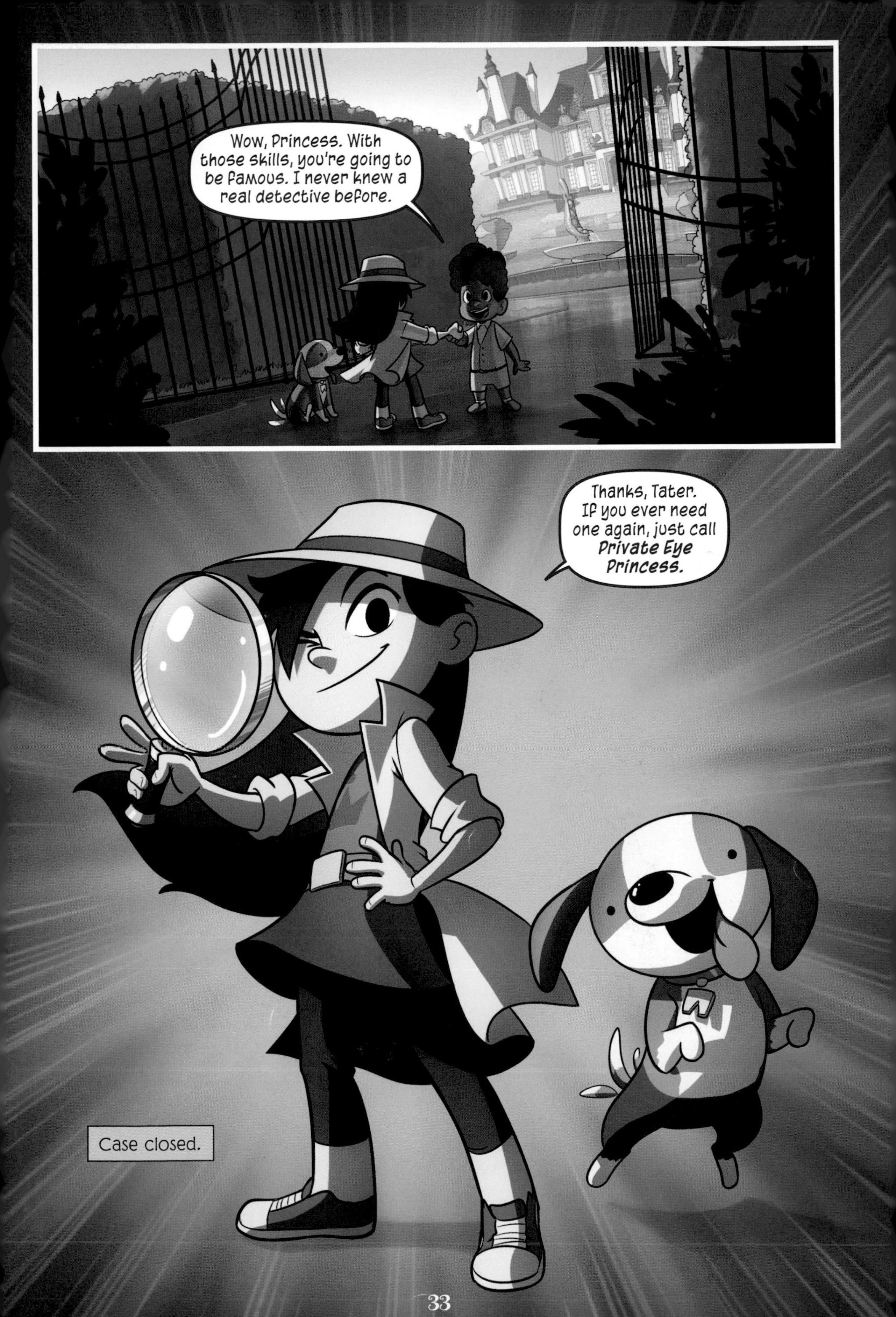
Wow, Princess. With those skills, you're going to be famous. I never knew a real detective before.
Thanks, Tater. If you ever need one again, just call *Private Eye Princess.*
Case closed.

ALL ABOUT THE ORIGINAL TALE!

Written in 1835 by Danish author Hans Christian Andersen, "The Princess and the Pea" isn't like most fairy tales. It doesn't feature the fantasy elements or magical creatures often found in these stories. But it does have a young woman with unusually strong senses.

The tale starts off with a prince looking to marry a princess. But he didn't want just any royal lady as his wife. He wanted a real, genuine princess. He searched all over the world but found only phony ones. The prince sadly returned home alone.

One night, during a terrible storm, a loud knocking came upon the palace door. The prince's father, the old king, answered. It was a young woman, completely drenched from the rain. Although she looked nothing like a princess, she said she was of noble blood.

The prince's mother, the old queen, doubted the visitor's claim. So she came up with a test to determine if the lady was telling the truth. The queen crept into the palace's guest bedroom and secretly placed a single pea beneath a stack of twenty soft mattresses. That evening the young woman fell back onto the mattresses, exhausted.

The next morning the queen asked if the lady had slept well. The young woman replied that she had been so uncomfortable that she barely closed her eyes all night and even had bruises from the lumpy bed. It was as if she'd been lying upon a rock!

Instantly, the queen, king, and prince knew that she must be a true princess—for only a princess could be so sensitive. And so the prince and the princess were married, living happily ever after.

A **FAR OUT** GUIDE TO
THE TALE'S MYSTERY TWISTS!

Instead of proving she's a true princess, this Princess proves she's a real detective!

The green pea has been swapped out for a missing emerald jewel.

In the original, the princess just has a rough night's sleep. Here Princess uses her sharp instincts and skills to find the pea.

Princess King doesn't get married in this version. (She's too young anyway!) Instead she impresses a big client and is one step closer to being a world-famous P.I.

VISUAL QUESTIONS

Princess is working the case at night during a storm, and many of the rooms are dark and shadowy. What feeling does this create as you read? How would the story be different if it took place during the day?

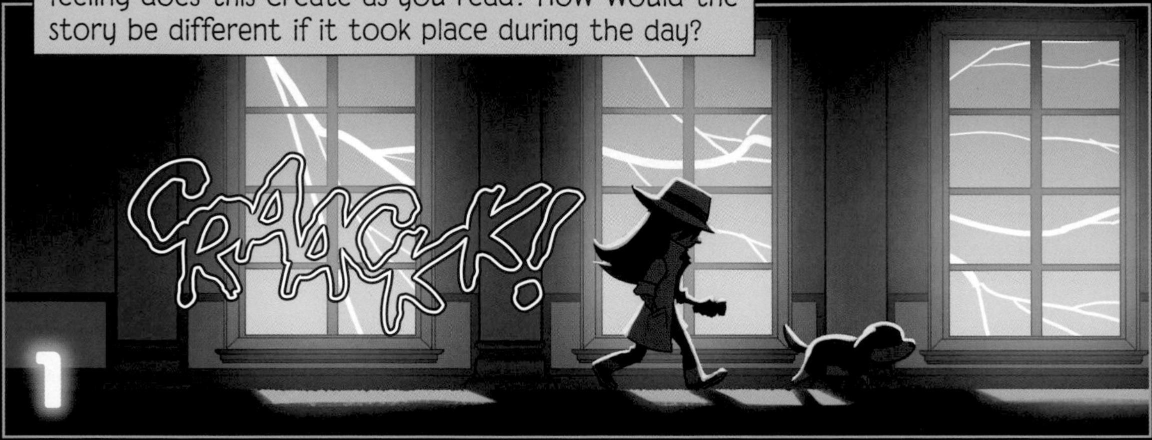

CRAACK!
1

Be a detective! Look closely at the art and text, and guess how Mini feels here. What makes you think that?

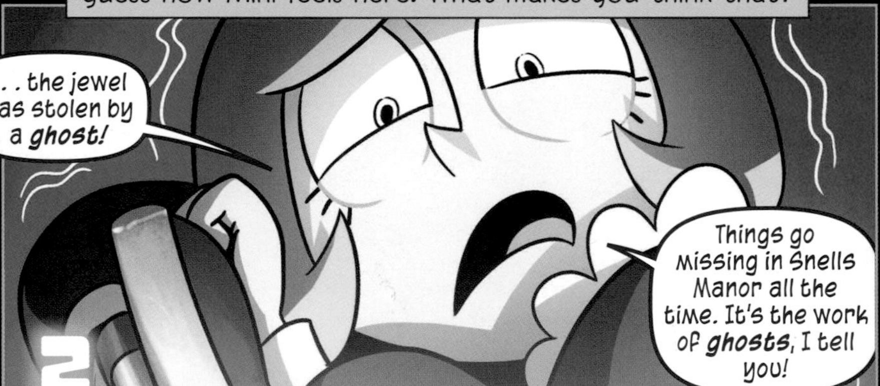

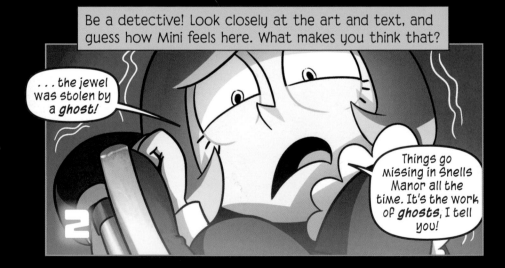

. . . the jewel was stolen by a ghost!
Things go missing in Snells Manor all the time. It's the work of ghosts, I tell you!
2

What is making the noise in the secret passageway? (Check pages 19 and 20 if you need help.)

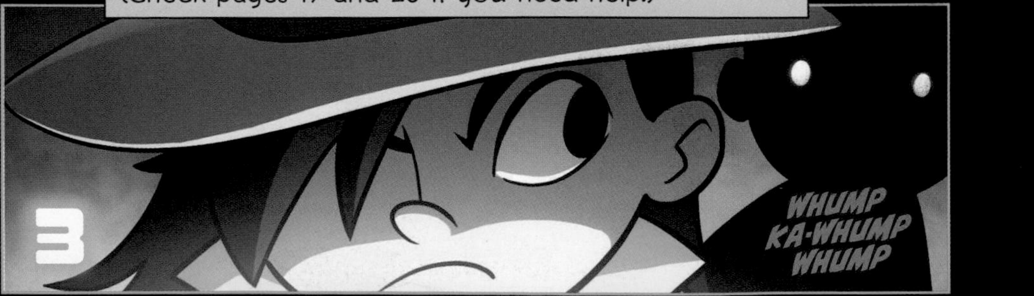

WHUMP KA-WHUMP WHUMP
3

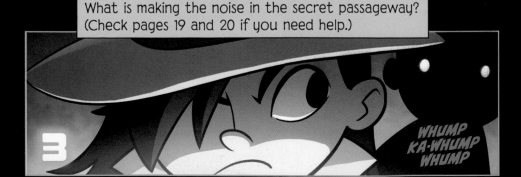

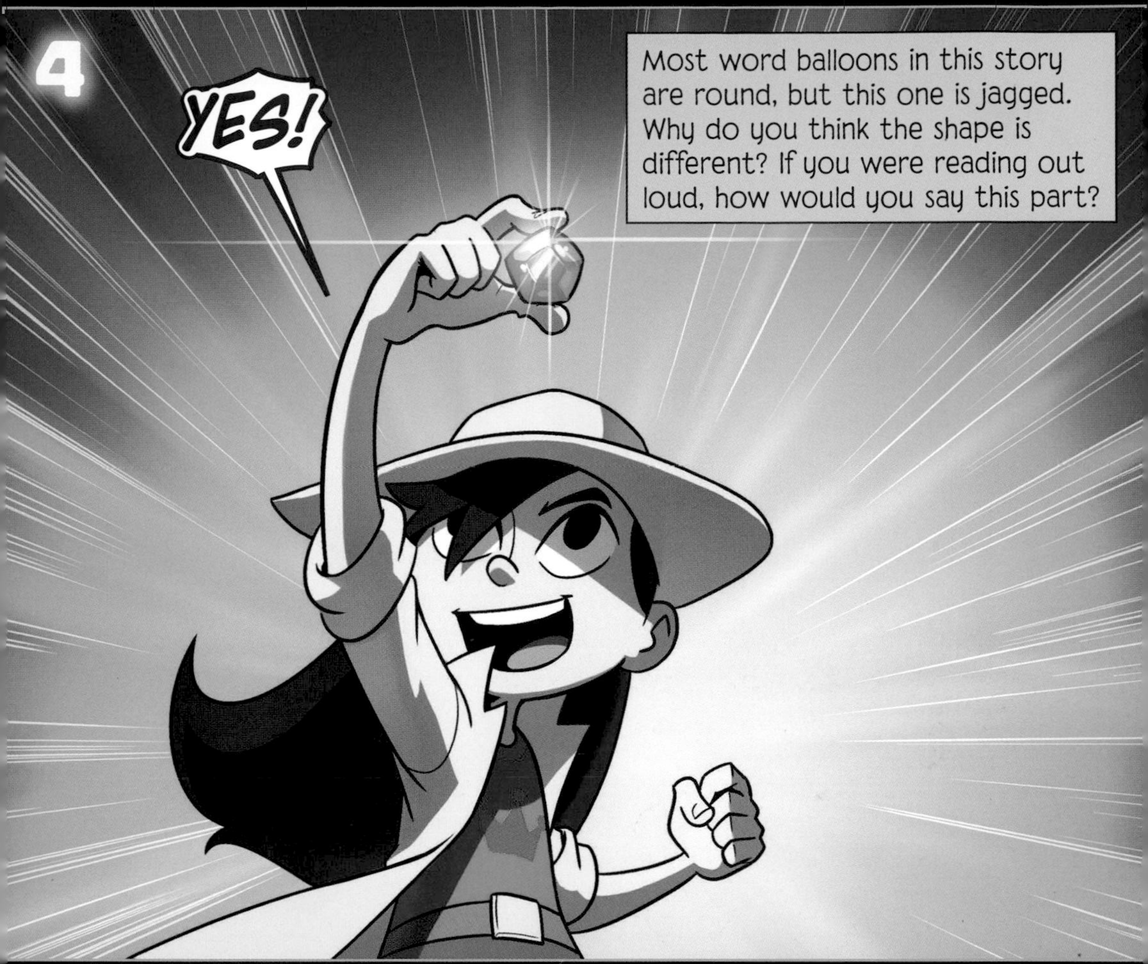
4
YES!
Most word balloons in this story are round, but this one is jagged. Why do you think the shape is different? If you were reading out loud, how would you say this part?

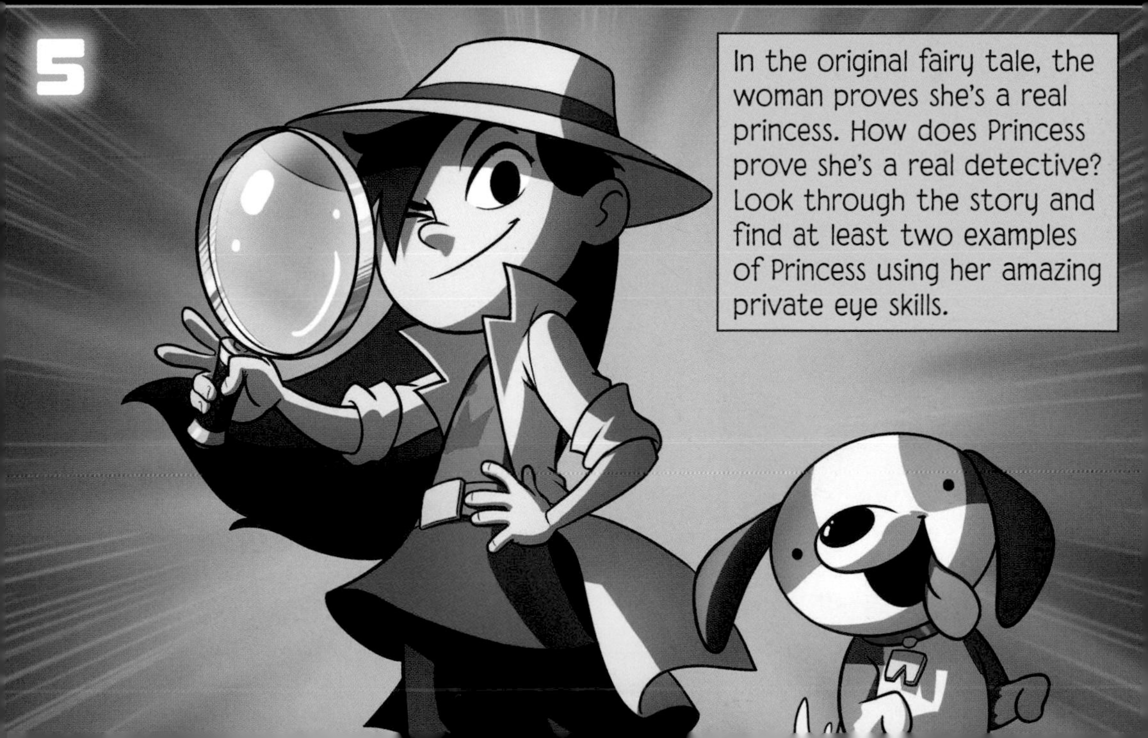
5
In the original fairy tale, the woman proves she's a real princess. How does Princess prove she's a real detective? Look through the story and find at least two examples of Princess using her amazing private eye skills.

AUTHOR

Martin Powell is the author of more than twenty children's books including *The Tall Tale of Paul Bunyan*, which won the national Moonbeam Gold Award for Best Children's Graphic Novel of 2010. Powell is the creator of The Halloween Legion, a nominee for the Stan Lee Excelsior Award, and also an educational writer for Gander Publishing, dedicated to improving literacy reading skills for students of all ages. In 2017, he received the coveted Golden Lion Award from The Burroughs Bibliophiles for his on-going contributions to the legacy of the adventure and sci-fi novelist Edgar Rice Burroughs.

ILLUSTRATOR

Fern Cano is an illustrator born in Mexico City, Mexico. He currently resides in Monterrey, Mexico, where he makes a living as an illustrator and colorist. He has done work for Marvel, DC Comics, and role-playing games like Pathfinder from Paizo Publishing. In his spare time, he enjoys hanging out with friends, singing, rowing, and drawing!

GLOSSARY

admit (ad-MIT)–to agree something is true, but often not wanting to say so

case (KAYS)–a set of events that needs to be studied and checked out by police (or a private investigator!)

examine (ig-ZAM-uhn)–to check very carefully

lookout (LOOK-out)–the act of watching carefully for something that is expected or feared

manor (MAN-er)–the main house on a large piece of land; usually a manor is a very big, expensive house

possibility (pos-uh-BIL-uh-tee)–something that might happen or be true

private investigator (PRY-vit in-VES-tuh-gay-tor)–a person who is not a member of the police but can be hired to gather information or look into possible crimes; also called a private eye or abbreviated as P.I.

proof (PROOF)–something that shows something else to be true

sensitive (SEN-si-tiv)–quickly able to notice small changes around you

solve (SAHLV)–to find the answer to a problem or mystery

valuable (VAL-yoo-buhl)–being worth a lot of money

wick (WIK)–the rope-like part of a candle or lamp that is lit

AWESOMELY EVER AFTER.

FAR OUT FAIRY TALES